Her coat gaped open, and Adam caught a glimpse of bare skin...

He blinked. It was freezing outside. Gracie couldn't be wearing nothing under that coat.

Could she?

"I hope whatever you're wearing under that didn't get ruined," he said casually, removing the wine-stained napkins from her lap. His heart did a back flip.

"It's okay." Gracie's sudden death grip on the coat told him all he needed to know. "It's red...what I'm wearing...underneath."

Adam swallowed. Her nervous tone told him he wasn't in this attraction alone. "Take off the coat, Gracie."

She jumped up. "I'll go upstairs and change."

Gently he took her hand and pulled her against him. She was warm and soft and totally giving. "Am I reading you wrong, Gracie?"

"No." Her eyes drifted closed, and a breathy sigh whispered from her lips. "I was trying to...I wanted to seduce you...."

ABOUT THE AUTHOR

A native of Hawaii, Debbi Rawlins married on Maui and has since lived in Cincinnati, Chicago, Tulsa, Houston, Detroit and Durham. One of her favorite things about living on the mainland is snow—she can't get enough of it! When Debbi isn't busy at the computer, she is usually lost in the pages of a book, or headed for the airport and parts unknown.

Books by Debbi Rawlins

HARLEQUIN AMERICAN ROMANCE

LOVE AND LAUGHTER

Don't miss any of our special offers. Write to us at the following address for information on our newest releases.

Harlequin Reader Service
U.S.: 3010 Walden Ave., P.O. Box 1325, Buffalo, NY 14269
Canadian: P.O. Box 609, Fort Erie, On t. L2A 5X3

Stud for Hire?

DEBBI RAWLINS

HARLEQUIN®

TORONTO • NEW YORK • LONDON
AMSTERDAM • PARIS • SYDNEY • HAMBURG
STOCKHOLM • ATHENS • TOKYO • MILAN • MADRID
PRAGUE • WARSAW • BUDAPEST • AUCKLAND

To my cousin, June Nelson—
a wonderful fan and friend.
Thanks for all your encouragement.
You're the best!

ISBN 0-373-16780-6

STUD FOR HIRE?

Copyright © 1999 by Debbi Quattrone.

Chapter One

"Maybe I should go blond." Gracie Louise Allen looked pensively past her friend and into her reflection in the coffee bar's wall mirror. It wasn't that she was having a bad hair day. Her hair looked the way it always did. Dull, mud-colored and unremarkable. Boring, actually. No wonder Dwight had quit paying attention to her. She sighed. "What do you think?"

Zoey stopped drumming her long glittering nails on the table and peered at Gracie over her rhinestone-studded glasses, which she wore for effect and not necessity. "You having a fat day?"

"No." Gracie stopped stirring sugar into her coffee and sucked in her tummy. The waistband of her navy skirt did feel a tad snug. She took a cautious breath and frowned. No doubt she could stand to lose five pounds. "Maybe."

Her friend grabbed the sugar Gracie had abandoned and dumped two more spoonfuls into her cup. "Okay, what's going on?"

"You're a hairdresser. I want to go blond. Would I have asked a plumber that question? No." Gracie slid the shaker of salt toward her and upended it over her coffee. "Nothing is going on."

Zoey propped her chin in her hand, eyed the salty coffee and grinned. "Uh-huh."

Gracie's shoulders sagged, and she pushed the cup aside. "Maybe blond is too radical. How about a few streaks? And a new haircut. Just enough to get the weight off my shoulders."

Zoey signaled the waitress for another cup, then leveled her concerned brown eyes on Gracie. "I'm your best friend. If you can't tell me, who are you gonna tell?"

That was part of the problem. Zoey was her best friend. She and her husband did everything with Gracie and Dwight. They were likely to take the news harder than Gracie had taken it. Breaking eye contact, she looked past Zoey and found herself staring at her reflection again. Her complexion was dull, tired.

"And maybe some blue contact lenses," she said absently. "Gray is so boring."

"You have perfect vision."

"That doesn't stop you."

"Yeah, but I have an image to protect." Zoey's chin came up. "You...you're..."

"Boring," Gracie finished.

"Conservative," Zoey said firmly.

Gracie's lips curved slightly at the fierce protectiveness she heard in her friend's voice, and she felt a little guilty for not having told her everything during the past year. She took a deep breath and said, "He moved out last night."

"Who?" Zoey's head reared back, her surprised

shriek netting them several abrupt glances from the other customers. "Dwight dumped you?"

Gracie felt rather than saw the stares of several more people as she leaned across the table. "Zoey, if you don't keep your voice down, so help me, I'll tell everyone in your salon that their hip boss is really a computer nerd."

She started to open her mouth again, but after seeing the I-mean-it look that Gracie had perfected over twenty years of friendship, Zoey settled back in her chair.

Leaning back, too, Gracie inhaled deeply, then offered a weak smile to a trio of women still looking her way. She knew most of the people in the coffee bar. The mall hadn't opened yet, and only other retail employees were indulging in a last moment of freedom before the shoppers descended.

Sniffing, Zoey adjusted her oversize black T-shirt until the red letters across her chest were legible. Take My Advice—I'm Not Using It.

"I can't believe it," Zoey said, her voice lowered. "After all these years. What a slime bucket. No, he's just stupid. I'll have Brian talk to him." One hand dived in agitation through her black hair before she waved it in the air. "We'll straighten this out in no time. As soon as Brian—"

"No, Zoey." Gracie shook her head. "It's over. And you can't tell me this is a surprise."

"Look, we all have those kinds of days. Brian and I argue, too."

"This isn't the same. We've been growing apart for a while. Most of the time he's more interested in his computer or whatever's on TV than he is in me."

"That doesn't mean anything."

Gracie held up a hand for silence. A bare hand. There should have been a ring on that finger by now, she thought with unexpected wistfulness. Promptly lowering her hand, she dragged her attention to Zoey…and her suspicious glare.

"You don't look very upset," Zoey said, her eyes narrowing. "It took you a half hour to spill the beans. Whose idea was it that he move out?"

Gracie adjusted the padded shoulders of her sensible navy blazer and sat straight in her chair. The action gave her an inch or two over Zoey, and a false confidence. She'd need every bit of it. "It was mutual."

Her friend's expression fell. "You kicked him out, didn't you?"

Gracie shook her head, sadness temporarily clogging her throat. She and Dwight had been together for five years, and the first three had been good. But the last two…well, they were too painful to think about right now.

"It was mutual. I promise. It's been coming for a long time. The only thing I'm guilty of is not telling you sooner how seriously wrong things were between us." She covered her friend's hand with hers. "I knew it was going to be tough on you and Brian. I'm sorry, kiddo."

Zoey blinked. "I am the world's biggest witch. You must feel like hell."

"Actually, I don't. It's kind of a relief. You know I've been wanting to buy into the boutique. Now I'll have plenty of time to work on doing that." She stopped and squeezed her friend's hand. "And you're not a witch. We've been a foursome for a long time. I expect you to be upset. Now, let's have some chocolate.''

''Aha.'' Zoey withdrew her hand and dived for the Flintstones lunch pail that served as her purse. ''I knew you were upset.''

''What?''

''You never eat chocolate before noon.''

Gracie grinned. ''There are a lot things you haven't seen me do. Maybe it's time I started kicking off my shoes, letting my hair down, going blond.''

''You? Yeah, right.'' Zoey broke her emergency bar in two and, after studying it for a second, passed the bigger piece to Gracie. ''Do you think if Brian were to talk to—''

''Zoey, stop. You're my best friend and I love you, but if you stick your big nose in this, I will think up some seriously juicy gossip about you to spread up one side of this mall and down the other.'' Although Gracie cringed inside, she held her ground. She hadn't meant to say it like that. Zoey was sensitive enough about her nose. ''I'm okay. Really.''

''Then why do you want to go blond? Or suddenly wear blue contacts? You're the most stable person I know. Probably the only stable person I know. This doesn't sound at all like you.'' Zoey shook her head and chomped into her chocolate. ''Not one bit.''

''I'm just trying to explore my options.''

''You're second-guessing yourself. That's what you're doing. You're feeling unattractive, and no matter whose idea it was to split up, you think this is mostly your fault.''

Gracie started to object but knew it would be useless. "How did you get so smart?"

"By listening to my customers. Half the time they think I'm a freakin' marriage counselor." Zoey eyed the candy Gracie had set aside. "Are you going to eat that?"

With the heel of her hand, Gracie slid the half a bar toward her. "It's all yours."

"I knew it." Zoey sighed, ignoring the chocolate, too. "You're in worse shape than I thought."

"You're wrong. It really isn't that bad. Dwight and I are still friends. We'll continue to do things together. In fact, we're still going to the concert with you and Brian tomorrow night."

Zoey's lips curved with hope, and her eyes lit up. "Maybe if you sent yourself flowers, Dwight would get jealous, and then…"

Gracie smiled, trying to be smart, sensible, steadfast…all the things she was noted for. But something in her expression obviously gave her away, because her friend's voice trailed off, and Zoey did something she never did. She gave up. She just sat there staring at Gracie with the most forlorn look on her face.

"Hey, you." Gracie leaned forward and shook her shoulder. "It's okay. It could have been worse. At least there's no divorce to worry about."

"Sure." Zoey tried to smile.

Gracie wished she could console her. She really did. But how could she explain to someone as blissfully happy as Zoey that the magic had died, that it may never have been there to begin with?

She bit her lip. That their relationship had been platonic for over a year now.

Zoey and Brian had been married for thirteen years, and they still acted like newlyweds. They laughed and touched a lot, exchanged knowing glances. Sometimes it was hard to double date with them. It reminded Gracie of everything she and Dwight had never shared.

"I'm looking forward to concentrating on buying the boutique," she said, that much certainly true. "Really. I've always wanted to be my own boss. You know that."

"Dwight always thought that was a dumb idea, huh? So that is one good thing about him not being around." Zoey made a face, and Gracie knew her friend didn't share Dwight's dim opinion. "Plus it always bugged you that he left his shoes wherever he took them off. You won't have to worry about that anymore," Zoey said, her lips beginning to curve.

"No kidding. And good riddance to all those water rings on the coffee table. In fact, I should make him take the damn table," Gracie said, laughing.

"Wow. You'll get the remote control all to yourself."

"The toilet seat will stay down."

"*And* you get to Christmas shop early and leave the stuff all over the house without anyone complaining."

"You do that, not me," Gracie reminded her. "I'm just looking forward to reading the newspaper while it's still in one piece."

Zoey sighed, slumped in her chair and picked up the rest of the chocolate bar. "Maybe I ought to kick Brian out. I could start Christmas shopping now."

Gracie chuckled. "You're so crazy about the guy you can't stand it when he leaves the room."

"Not quite." Zoey laughed, then bit into the candy, her expression growing pensive. "It was never like that for you and Dwight, was it?"

And then Gracie saw it. Exactly what she didn't want to see. Pity darkened Zoey's eyes. It etched itself between her friend's dark brows. It turned down the corners of her mouth. It stretched between years of friendship, and it made Gracie feel horrible for being so envious of her friend's healthy marriage.

Because the odds had been in Gracie's favor, not Zoey's, and Gracie didn't understand why she wasn't the one happily married and planning a family. She'd played by the rules all her life. She'd been the good daughter, the good employee. She'd always done what was expected of her.

Zoey hadn't. Zoey had been the rebel, the one voted most likely to skip town and join the circus. So where had Gracie gone so wrong? Why wasn't the ring on *her* finger?

She certainly didn't blame Zoey, but she didn't want to discuss the sordid details of her screwed-up life, either.

"Look, I've got to get to the store and open. I'm the only one there until noon," she said, grabbing her purse. And then she saw anxiety replace pity on Zoey's face, and she hesitated. "Are we still on for lunch?"

"Sure." Zoey's shrug was nonchalant, but she looked relieved. She laid a hand on Gracie's forearm when Gracie started to get up. "It's not you. You do know that, don't you?"

"I know."

Zoey frowned. "Do you?"

That's what was so hard. Dwight was a boring guy. He always had been, and even he wouldn't dispute it. She'd never really minded. But now, *she* had bored him. That hurt. She swallowed, then smiled. "Like you said, the guy's an idiot."

"Right. So don't start getting weird on me."

"Moi?" Gracie asked, and they both laughed.

"Streaks may be okay, but not totally blond. We'll talk about it at lunch."

"I won't do anything rash in the meantime."

Zoey grinned. "I'm counting on that." And then her lips pulled into a straight line. "We'll talk later, huh?"

"Sure. We'll talk," Gracie said to reassure her. Not that she had any intention of discussing the painful and mentally debilitating breakdown of her relationship with Dwight. Zoey wouldn't understand. Grace didn't, either.

ADAM KNIGHT had barely edged onto the black lacquered bar-style stool when the dark-haired waitress set a cup of strong, kick-you-in-the-gut Colombian java in front of him. This was only the third time he'd been to this coffee bar, and he smiled at her, impressed that she'd remembered his preference.

"Thanks, Betty," he said, glancing at her name tag.

"Any time, sugar. Now, maybe you'd like a little something sweet to go with that?" She gave him a saucy wink and leaned forward, her cleavage oozing out of her cotton-candy pink uniform.

One corner of Adam's mouth lifted in a wry salute. Even at thirty-four he remembered when women had waited for a man to ask. "Well, darlin', you'll be the first to know."

"You just give me a holler any time." As she straightened she adjusted her name tag, drawing his attention once again to the plump mounds of pale flesh framed by her crisp white lapels.

Adam let his gaze linger a moment before he unfolded his newspaper, set aside his cup, and spread the paper open to the classified section.

There weren't many construction jobs listed, and he found the ad he'd placed right away. He studied it to check for accuracy until the weight of someone's stare pricked the back of his neck and made him as uneasy as a buck in season.

The mall had just opened, and Cup-A-Chinos was nearly empty. Slowly, reluctantly, he raised his gaze, expecting to find Betty offering another blatant invitation.

Across the narrow room was a woman in a black T-shirt with red writing that he couldn't quite make out scrawled across the front.

She frowned slightly behind ridiculous rhinestone, cat's-eye glasses and made no attempt to avert her eyes. Her Cleopatra-style hair was unnaturally black against her pale complexion. She looked like some sort of Anne Rice groupie.

He smiled briefly, hoping she'd realize she'd been caught staring and buzz off. But she merely chewed on her bright red lips and frowned harder.

Adam exhaled a deep, audible breath and returned his attention to the newspaper. He was in desperate need of workers before the bad weather hit. He couldn't count on Indian summer. October would be here next week, and that meant unpredictable conditions. He'd contracted three other jobs in southern Ohio in the past four years, and because of unexpected cold snaps, each time he'd met his deadline by the skin of his teeth.

If he weren't careful, this one would be no exception. Except that foul weather represented only a fraction of the odds stacked against him. This mall extension job was already seriously behind schedule. That's why the mall owner had brought him in, why the man had offered him such a sweet deal if he finished on time. If he didn't, this job was going to cost Adam a lot of money out of his own pocket.

Although that wasn't what concerned him. He could always make more money. His reputation, however, was something he didn't mess with. They called him the miracle worker within the construction industry. He was the guy they called when all else failed. So far, he had a perfect record of rescuing failing projects. He had no intention of changing that statistic. His exorbitant fee was a fringe benefit, but the truth was, he liked winning.

Adam checked his watch, then started folding the paper. He figured anyone responding to the ad would start showing up at the job site within the hour.

"Excuse me."

His hand stilled over his cup. Before turning toward the feminine voice over his shoulder, he motioned for the waitress to bring him a coffee to go. He hoped that gave his visitor a hint.

"Yes?" He summoned a half smile as he slid off

the stool, then angled around to look at the woman who had been staring. His mama had taught him a lot of things he didn't want to think about, but she'd also taught him not to be rude. "What can I do for you?"

"Plenty." Ignoring his hint, she slid onto the stool next to him. "I couldn't help noticing that you were looking for a job. I have one for you."

Adam blinked, then he laughed. "What?"

"It's nothing big and it'll probably only last for a couple of weeks, but it won't take much of your time, either, so you can be looking for something more permanent."

Up close she was kind of pretty, but obviously batty as they come. He couldn't help but wonder what kind of job she had in mind as his gaze traveled up her leopard-print leggings to her mop of thick black hair. "I'm not looking for a job."

Her dramatically made-up face softened. "I didn't mean to embarrass you. We've all been out of work from time to time. No shame in that."

The waitress plopped a cup in front of him. "Anything else, Adam?" she asked in an irritatingly sweet voice while sliding a speculative look at the other woman.

He frowned. It was Adam now? He didn't remember telling her his name. When had women started getting so pushy? "Uh, no, thanks." He pulled his wallet out of his back pocket.

"Never mind." Betty laid her palm across his forearm, and as far as he was concerned, left it there ten seconds too long. "*She* already got it."

He felt his blood pressure climb as he turned to his table companion. "Wait a minute."

"See ya, Betty." The woman wiggled her fingers at the waitress. When Betty disappeared in a huff behind the counter, his unwelcome companion faced him and shrugged. "She's new."

He finished fishing the wallet out of his pocket and laid several bills on the table. "I believe this ought to cover it."

"No, please, it's on me. It's the least I can do for taking up your time. I'm Zoey Mulrooney, by the way." She stuck out her hand, her nails glittering with some silver sparkly stuff.

"Zoey, I'm sure you're a very nice person and you mean well but I'm not interested—"

"Oh, I'm not the one you have to kiss up to."

His eyebrows rose. "I'm supposed to kiss up to someone?"

"Yeah." She lowered her voice, glanced around the room, then leaned across the table. "My friend Gracie. But she can't know anything about it."

"Why does your friend need someone to kiss up to her?" he asked, wondering why in the hell he had. This woman was obviously a nut. Except she not only looked dead serious but a little distressed, and he couldn't quite bring himself to walk away.

"Because she's feeling really low right now." Zoey sighed, her entire body sagging. She propped her arm on the table and let her chin sink into her palm. "She's this really great person who's always there for everyone. She'd give you her last cent, and she'd probably even clean the house for you if you asked her. Which is way more than I can fathom." She stopped and frowned. "Well, not *you* specifically, but, well, probably even you...a total stranger. Because that's just the kind of person she is. And now Dwight's being a jerk.''

"Ah, Dwight's the boyfriend," he said, nodding. As scary a prospect as it was, the woman was starting to make sense.

"*Was* the boyfriend, but I think we can fix that. What do ya say?''

Adam took a step back. And stopped. "What's her name?''

"Gracie. Gracie Allen.''

"Like the comedienne?''

She nodded. "Her mother wanted her to always have a sense of humor.''

"And does she?''

"Are you kidding?'' She pushed the rhinestone glasses up the bridge of her nose, looking mildly appalled. "You have to have sense of humor to be my friend,'' she said, and Adam wasn't quite sure how to take that. "And she's smart, too. Graduated first in her class from OU.''

He frowned. *Great.* Just what he needed. "One of those academic types, huh?''

"Not hardly. She's the manager of Something Wicked here in the mall.''

"That sex shop?''

Zoey laughed. "It's not a sex shop. It's a woman's boutique. She'd faint if she heard you say that. She's sort of—'' She stopped, scrunching up her face. "How shall I put this? Old-fashioned isn't the right word.'' Her forehead creased in concentration. "Conservative is close enough.''

"Old-fashioned, huh?'' He rubbed his jaw. He couldn't remember the last time he'd met a woman like that. Out of the corner of his eye, he saw Betty lurking behind the counter. Old-fashioned would certainly be a refreshing change.

"Not old-fashioned," Zoey said quickly. "God, don't tell her she's old-fashioned. You have to make her feel...hot."

"Hot," he repeated dryly.

"Yeah. And make sure Dwight sees you flirting with her. Then he'll realize what a stupid dweeb he is for walking out on the best thing that ever happened to him."

Adam chuckled. He was starting to feel a little sorry for the guy. Zoey obviously wasn't someone to mess with. But he did admire her fierce devotion to her friend. "And you think that will work?"

"I hope so," she said gravely. "They've been together too long to let everything get shot to hell now."

"You're either a really good friend or a total nutcase, Zoey Mulrooney."

She grinned. "You'll do it?"

He wondered what the old-fashioned, conservative Gracie Allen would say if she knew her friend had just revealed Gracie's life history.

"I really wasn't looking for a job," he said, surprised that he found himself even thinking about getting involved in this crazy scheme.

She smiled as though she didn't believe him, and he told himself to walk out right now. He had concrete to mix, supplies to order and, he hoped, a busload of men to interview. He was already behind schedule.

Picking up his cup, he shook his head. *He* was the

nutcase for even giving this deal passing consideration.

"By the way, you'll need this." After rooting through a child's lunch pail, Zoey plucked out a burgundy wallet, withdrew a small snapshot and handed it to him. "That's Gracie next to me," she said.

Adam stared at the picture and put his cup on the table. Although Zoey had red spiky hair in this photo, he quickly identified her. Then his gaze fell on the image of the woman beside her.

He noticed her smile first. It was wide and genuine, and she looked comfortable with it, as though she smiled a lot. Her eyes were attractive, too. Although he couldn't tell what color they were, they looked bright and sincere, and he instantly understood her friend's obvious loyalty.

"She's pretty," he said, promptly passing back the photograph.

"Of course she is." Zoey beamed like a proud parent, and he decided right then that he liked her. "Don't forget smart, too."

"It shouldn't be too hard to find someone for the job."

Zoey's eyes widened. "You're backing out?"

"Look," he said, rotating a stiff shoulder, trying to work out the achy feeling settling in, and wondered if it was a sign the cold weather would be here early. "I'm sure there's someone more suitable. I really don't have the time."

"No," Zoey concluded with an emphatic shake of her head. "You know too much. If I don't use you now, I'll have to kill you."

"Excuse me?"

"Just kidding. Sort of." She leaned forward and caught his arm. It wasn't a sexual touch, not like Betty's. It was a desperate one. "Adam, I need you. Name your price."

Her voice had risen in her excitement, and Adam cringed over how that sounded. He quickly scanned the room.

Three women pushed through the doors of the coffee bar, but they were too busy laughing and talking to pay him any attention. Looking out the plate-glass windows, Adam saw that the mall had started to fill up with shoppers. He wondered if he could get out of Cup-A-Chinos without Zoey making a scene.

His gaze fell on her long silvery nails and the death grip she had on him, and then his attention wandered to Gracie Allen's picture lying in the center of the table.

She had an incredible smile.

Yup. Zoey wouldn't have any trouble finding someone at all.

Hell, who was he kidding? He wanted to do it. Besides, he was the miracle worker, right? The guy they called when the chips were down. Surely he could handle a little harmless flirtation. He'd get the two lovebirds back together and feel like a Good Samaritan. No problem.

"Tell me something," he said. "Why me?"

He was immediately sorry he asked. Zoey started to smile while eyeing him like he was a sizzling steak hot off the grill. He flexed his arm and escaped her hold, but her gaze stayed fastened on him as if she was a starving woman.

About the time he had serious thoughts of crawling

under the table, she said, "Because you're gorgeous and Dwight will feel like a toad next to you." Her eyes narrowed to glittering slits, and she added, "And besides my husband, you've got the best buns I've seen in years." He jumped when she reached around him, but all she did was slip something—probably the picture—into his back pocket.

Adam massaged his throbbing temple, watching as Zoey rushed out of the shop. Old-fashioned was starting to sound better by the minute.

Chapter Two

Gracie realized an hour too late that she had to be out of her mind. What had gotten into her that she had allowed Zoey free rein with a partial makeover?

She peered at herself in the beauty shop mirror and grimaced. Her face was all lips. She blotted the coral-colored lipstick a third time. It didn't help. The color remained stubbornly bright and screamed, ''Look at me.''

The eye makeup wasn't too bad, though. Even without the benefit of contacts, her eyes looked more blue than gray thanks to several subtle layers of plum shadow.

''Hey, keep still or I won't finish in time for this to dry and we'll be late for the concert.'' Zoey lightly pinched Gracie's ankle for emphasis, then wiggled into a more comfortable position on the floor cushion she was sitting on before going back to polishing Gracie's toenails.

That got Gracie's attention, all right. She squinted at Zoey's artillery. ''What color is that?''

''Mauve,'' Zoey said with so much innocence that Gracie knew she was in trouble.

"The other one. What's the bottle next to it?"

"Go back to blotting. I'll tell you when you can look again."

"I knew you were up to something." Gracie moved her foot, and the brush awkwardly swept sunset mauve across the fleshy tips of three toes.

"You're going to make us late."

"No, I'm not. We're done."

Zoey let out a long-suffering sigh. "You beg me to make you blond, then you complain about a little glitter way down here where no one can see it."

"I can see it. And it looks gauche."

The bottle was the same color as Zoey's nails. She gave Gracie a dirty look.

"It's just not me, okay? I'd rather you'd made me a blonde."

"Your hair is too pretty as it is. I charge a hundred bucks to give people that honey-toned hue," Zoey said, and vigorously rubbed the polish off Gracie's toes.

"Ouch. There's skin under there, you know."

"Tough. We're going to be late."

"Since when are you worried about being late?" Gracie asked, and leaned forward to keep closer tabs on what was happening with her pedicure.

"Relax. Thanks to your little two-step, we only have time for one coat of mauve. We have to meet Brian and Dwight at Cup-A-Chinos in five minutes."

"I still don't understand why we're meeting them there. It doesn't make sense." Gracie glanced at her watch, then frowned at Zoey. It hadn't occurred to her until this moment that Dwight might think all this primping was for him. "I hope he doesn't show up."

Zoey lost control of the brush and sent a spray of color across the black and white tiled beauty shop floor. She looked anxiously at Gracie. "Who?"

She blinked. "Dwight. Who else?"

"Oh." Zoey swiped a rag across the floor. "We're all done. Why don't you want him to show up?"

"I can't put my sandals back on yet. They'll mess up the polish."

"I'll carry them for you. You can put them on at Cup-A-Chinos. Do you think he won't show up?"

"I can't walk barefoot down the mall." Gracie slid out of the chair but refused to follow Zoey to the door.

"You said you wanted to start living dangerously," Zoey said, rolling her eyes and doubling back to grab Gracie's arm. She jerked her forward and Gracie quit arguing and let herself be dragged out of the salon.

"Dwight's going to think I did all this for him," she said. "That's the last thing I want."

"Trust me, Gracie, you don't look all that different."

"I never wear coral lipstick."

"Living life on the edge is nerve-racking, isn't it?"

"I don't wear dresses this short, either," Gracie added, then laughed despite her protests, while ignoring a middle-aged couple ogling her feet. It felt strangely liberating to be traipsing down the center of Oak City Mall wearing nothing but a short denim dress and a coat of mauve. The old Gracie wouldn't have done that. "Hey, I'm even wearing sandals in September."

Zoey dangled the bronze strappy slippers in front of her and grinned. "Only if I give them back," she said, and slipped through the glass doors of the coffee bar.

Gracie took another look at her mauve toenails, then followed her friend inside. The narrow room was almost filled to capacity. For the nearly eight years she'd worked at the mall, Gracie had hung out here with Zoey. The place had changed hands twice, but only recently had it become known as the new yuppie hangout. Gracie missed the days when they could come in for a quick cup of coffee or a quiet cappuccino.

She sighed. It seemed like everything was changing these days.

"Zoey," she hissed from just inside the door. Three customers besides Zoey turned to look at her. Zoey seemed distracted, and after glancing only briefly at Gracie, she focused her attention on the room. Gracie already could see that the guys weren't there yet, so she waited impatiently for her friend to turn around again. When she finally did, she waved her over.

"I can't come in here like this. It's probably against some health law or something," Gracie said, and tried to snag the sandals.

Zoey jerked them out of reach, her gaze continuing to scan the crowd. "Darlene isn't going to kick us out. We're her best customers. Sit at a table near the door if it makes you feel better."

"I think I can slip them on without messing up the polish."

Zoey lifted her chin in that stubborn tilt Gracie knew far too well and pointed at a chair. "I'll get our cappuccinos. Darlene looks busy."

"We don't have time for cappuccinos."

"Sure we do," Zoey said, glancing out the door. She slipped away before Gracie could argue.

Gracie found the last empty table and sank into one of the two chairs. Luckily, the table was near the door and in a deserted corner, so she settled back, stretched out her legs and stared at her toes. She wiggled them, and the sleek polish caught the overhead light, making her nails shimmer. She tried to remember when she'd had her last pedicure, or manicure, for that matter. She couldn't.

It was amazing how in the past five years, she hadn't made time for even the simplest things in her life. She'd been so caught up in absorbing Dwight's moods, his feelings, that she'd turned into nothing more than an emotional sponge. She was relieved that chapter in her life was over.

She grinned and straightened. She really was relieved. And she didn't care if Dwight did think she'd put on the dog for him. In fact, she wasn't going to think about Dwight at all.

Sighing, she stretched out and gazed happily at the luster of her flexed toes. It wasn't just a coat of mauve nail enamel, she decided, it was the symbol of her new liberated self. The one who was going to start living life a little more selfishly. The one who just might surprise the heck out of Zoey by wearing the stash of boutique clothes Zoey didn't think Gracie had the guts to wear. The thought appealed to her immensely.

She supposed that's why she didn't see him coming.

Everything happened so fast. The table clattered

from absorbing his weight when he grabbed it, trying to dodge her outstretched legs. The steel toe of his battered work boot grazed her shin, and she grimaced more from surprise than pain.

He swiveled to avoid taking down the table and nearly landed in her lap. Instead, he swiveled again and smoothly glided into the empty chair across from her as though he'd meant to sit there in the first place. Several onlookers clapped. He bowed his head in their direction as one corner of his mouth twitched.

When his eyes finally met hers, his dark brows drew together in either surprise or irritation, she couldn't tell which.

Gracie felt the heat climb her neck and bloom in her face. Quickly she drew in her legs. She opened her mouth to apologize, but her tongue felt heavier than a three-pound summer sausage and only a squeaky pathetic croak made it past her lips.

The stranger grinned, tanned skin crinkling at the corners of his velvety brown eyes. "Thanks for saving me a seat," he said, winking. "Have you ordered already?"

Gracie thought twice about trusting her ability to speak, so she merely nodded.

"Adam Knight." He stuck out his hand.

She took a deep breath, then she took his hand. His palm was slightly rough and callused, and it made hers feel a little prickly and hot. It had to be the recent manicure, she told herself, and yanked her hand back to the safety of her own space.

"Gracie," she said. "Gracie Klutz."

He smiled again, showing off perfect white teeth, and then her stomach got all prickly and hot, too.

"It's nice to meet you, Gracie…Klutz. Mind if I sit here?"

"Well…" She twisted in her chair and found Zoey behind the counter laughing with Darlene and whacking the side of the cappuccino machine. "I have a friend here with me," she said, turning to him and she had to force herself to remember to breathe.

He'd leaned back in the chair and looked totally at ease, his pale blue T-shirt stretching across a broad chest that was clearly defined beneath the thin material. The shirt really wasn't tight except around the arms, where the sleeves strained against rounded muscles. He wasn't one of those yuppie types who frequented the coffee bar, and she doubted he'd earned those muscles in some chic gym.

She remembered the slightly rough texture to his hands, and her tongue did that odd little swelling number again. "Do you work out?" she asked while she still could.

He rubbed his chest in a purely male gesture while appearing to give the question some thought.

Gracie briefly closed her eyes. *Do you work out?* She was going to give herself a good swift kick in the rear…the heck with the pedicure.

She breathed deeply, then smiled brightly. "I only ask because there's an aerobics studio here in the mall. They have several different classes from beginning to advanced. I teach intermediate twice a week. I just do it part time because I enjoy it." She shrugged helplessly, horrified at her babbling. "I better go help my friend Zoey," she said, and shot off her chair.

"Let me," he said, rising and looking pointedly at her feet.

"Oh." Gracie's gaze followed his. She wiggled her toes nervously. "Did I tell you I was sorry about tripping you?"

"I figured the invitation covered that."

She frowned. "What invitation?"

"To join your aerobics class," he said, and headed for the counter.

At first, Adam chuckled at her shocked expression, but as he got several feet away, reality hit him and he cursed under his breath. What was he doing? He didn't have time to go jump around in some aerobics class. Especially with a bunch of women. He shuddered at the thought of rows and rows of Stepford Bettys bouncing around in skimpy leotards. As much as he might enjoy the view, he didn't want to have to take anyone to the dance.

And in his experience, that would inevitably become an issue.

Of course, he didn't have to show up at aerobics. Although that would probably end up being a moot point. He had a feeling Gracie Allen wasn't going to roll out the welcome mat, no matter how cleverly he accepted her backhanded invitation. Oddly, that didn't cheer him.

He had to smile, though, when he thought about her. About the way she blushed clear to her hairline. Women didn't do that much anymore.

When he got to the counter, Zoey stopped fussing with the cappuccino machine and darted a frantic look at Gracie. "Pretend you don't know me," she whispered and started to turn to the machine.

Adam stuck out his hand. "Adam Knight," he said

calmly, and with a wary and confused expression, Zoey accepted the handshake. "I'm a friend of Gracie's," he continued, jerking a thumb over his shoulder in her direction.

It was impossible for Gracie to hear them. He merely went through the motions to enhance the charade. So when Zoey angled her head to look at her friend, he turned and waved at Gracie. Her hand shot up in a nervous gesture, but instead of waving she pushed the hair away from her face.

"Can I carry anything back to the table?" he asked, his gaze turned steadily and purposefully on Zoey.

She received the message loud and clear. This was part of the game. As far as anyone was concerned, they'd just met. He suddenly wondered where Betty was, but when he skimmed the room, he didn't see her. She was on the morning shift, he reminded himself.

"Sure...what did you say your name was?"

He smiled. "Adam."

"Take these to Gracie, would ya?" She passed him a pair of women's sandals. "These napkins, too. I'll bring the cappuccinos as soon as I get this freakin' machine to work."

"Right." He stuffed the sandals in the back pocket of his jeans and returned to the table.

"You have something for me?" Gracie asked with raised eyebrows after he'd sat and placed the napkins on the table. Her tawny hair was slightly curly and kept fluttering in wisps near her cheeks. She unconsciously blew at it, an action he found both arousing and distracting.

She cleared her throat.

"Your friend is having trouble with the cappuccino machine."

"I can see that." She put out her palm. "My sandals, please."

"Why weren't you wearing them?" he asked, making no move to hand them over.

"Because my nails were wet."

His gaze fell to her outstretched hand. He reached for it and turned it over to inspect her nails.

She laughed. "Not those."

Instead of releasing her hand, he ducked his head to look under the table. Gracie had nice legs. Better than nice. All those aerobics classes had certainly paid off.

She uncrossed and recrossed her legs and tugged her hand free. "Someone just left. If you hurry you can grab their table."

"Do we need a bigger table?" he asked, and met her distressed gaze. She was clearly trying to figure out how to be tactful yet get him to leave. Checking a grin, he pulled the sandals out of his pocket to distract her.

It worked like a charm. She smiled and held out her hand again.

He hunkered down in front of her and easily circled her ankle with his hand. Her skin was smoother than expensive silk sheets, and he felt a sudden pull in his gut that was going to get him butt-deep in trouble if he didn't wise up. "I promise you won't get a scratch on your toes."

Even when she flexed her foot, looking for escape, he kept a firm hold with plenty of room to spare. "Mr. Knight," she whispered frantically. "I can do that myself."

"I think we're a little past the Mr. Knight stage. Hold still."

"We're not at any stage. I don't even know you."

"We can change that. Have dinner with me tomorrow night."

He almost dropped the sandals the instant the words left his mouth. He and Zoey hadn't agreed on an actual date. They were going to stick to chance meetings…and only when Dwight was around.

"I have a boyfriend," she blurted, her hands clutching the side of the chair so tightly that her knuckles paled.

Slowly he slipped a sandal on her right foot, carefully arranging the straps so they cleared her purple-colored toenails. It wasn't easy because her toes kept curling, and he didn't trust himself to open his big mouth right now.

He couldn't go to dinner with her, and he was going to accept the out she gave him, but he'd have to do it gently. If he sounded too eager, she'd know he already regretted the invitation.

The heel of her foot fit perfectly in his palm, and the skin there was incredibly soft. He hadn't known it was possible for feet to be that soft, and he moved his hand to get a better feel.

A low, strangled sound came from Gracie, and

when he looked up she was glaring at him. "Don't," she said sternly, then giggled. "I mean it."

"What?" He let his palm graze the entire bottom of her foot. "This?" He'd never thought himself the type to be susceptible to fetishes, but a wild fantasy rooted itself in his brain, and the rest of his body was having trouble dealing with the vivid images of Gracie's pale nude body framed by black silk sheets.

He dropped her foot and handed her the other sandal. "Not a scratch," he said, and took his chair.

He rubbed the back of his neck. "So you have this boyfriend, huh?"

Gracie's eyes were still wide, and the blush hadn't subsided from her face. Her mouth was formed in a slight O, and he suddenly wanted to see that great smile she had.

He wasn't going to get it. Her lips quivered then pressed into a thin line of irritation. Whereas her eyes had looked blue before, they had darkened to a stormy gray.

"Mr. Knight," she said, "I suggest you take that other table while you still can."

He studied her for a moment and was amazed to realize that she was really angry. "The boyfriend's coming?" he asked.

"This has nothing to do with him." She leaned forward and slipped the other sandal on her foot without regard for her toes. Then she straightened and with narrowed eyes added, "I don't know what kind of women you're accustomed to, but I don't appreciate your liberties."

Adam stared at her. She sounded just like his tight-assed mother and all her highfalutin university friends. He'd underestimated her. She certainly was no shrinking violet.

He didn't know what to think about Gracie Allen anymore.

"Well, excuse me for trying to help." He raked a hand through his hair and looked away. He could leave right now. Zoey would hear the story from Gracie and know her plan wasn't going to work.

"I am sorry for causing you to trip, and I appreciate your being a good sport about it. I also appreciate your bringing my sandals," she said, her gentle tone compelling him to look at her again. "But surely you can't think I'd appreciate a perfect stranger touching me."

Her cheeks were still tinged with pink, and she looked uncomfortable bringing this up. But that didn't keep her from standing her ground. She lifted her chin, then her eyebrows, then she leaned back in her chair waiting for his reaction.

A vicious curse echoed in his head. She was right, of course. Why should he have presumed to touch her? He was being as bad as those pushy women who drove him nuts. His only defense was that he felt like he did know her a little. He'd looked at her picture several times yesterday and several more today, and he'd thought a lot about the things Zoey had told him. But Gracie didn't know all that. To her, he was a perfect stranger.

"You're right," he said, "I apologize."

She smiled. The same smile that had originally

hooked him into this mess. "Okay." She fidgeted with her hands, moistened her lips. "So, you—"

"You have—"

They both spoke at the same time and laughed. "You go first," she said.

"I wanted to know when you taught aerobics."

Her hands started fidgeting again. "Uh, Tuesdays and Thursdays."

"Evenings?"

Her expression crumpled. "You aren't seriously thinking of coming to class, are you?"

"Whoa, you don't pull any punches."

She blinked, then looked over her shoulder. Presumably to look for Zoey, who was still busy with the cappuccino machine. "It's just that there are only women in the class. I don't think you'd be very comfortable there."

"Around women? I'm very comfortable around them."

"Yes." She blew at her hair. The stray tendrils fluttered around her face before settling on her cheeks. "I'm sure you are, but we take fitness very seriously—"

He clutched his chest as though wounded. "Don't I look like I take fitness seriously?"

The rosiness seeped into her complexion again as her gaze fell to his arms. Then she raised her eyes to meet his and said, "I don't know. Can I feel your abs?"

He chuckled. She could have knocked him over with a feather. He briefly considered reminding her they were strangers, then decided to call her bluff instead. "With or without the shirt?" He grasped the hem.

"With is fine," she said, and leaning forward, she barely gave him time to suck it in before she pressed her palm against his belly. "Not bad."

"Not bad?" he drawled, inclining his head in disbelief. "Give me a break."

She grinned. "Okay, better than average."

He frowned. "Let me feel yours."

Her brows shot up. "You did enough feeling for one day," she said, and settled out of reach. "Besides, I did that out of professional interest."

"Enough for one day, huh?" A slow grin tugged at his mouth. "Does that mean we get to do this again?"

Her forehead creased briefly, then she laughed. "No, leave my feet alone."

As nice and soft as they were, her feet weren't what he had in mind, but he wasn't going to tell her *that*. "Back to my abs," he said instead. "So in your professional opinion, I'm above average?"

Her lips started to curve. "Well…let's see…on a scale of one to ten?"

He wasn't sure he wanted to get rated. "You're not going to hold it against me that I don't hang out in one of those yuppie gyms."

"I might hold it against you if you did."

He grinned, liking her all over again.

"Don't you want to know what your rating is?"

His smile faded. "That depends on—"

He didn't have to worry about answering her after all. Her anxious gaze had drifted to a spot behind him, and he could tell she wasn't listening to a word he said. He twisted around to see what had so raptly caught her attention.

Two men were entering the coffee bar. One had red hair, the other blond. Preppy haircuts and glasses. Mid-thirties.

He frowned, turning to her. He was about to say something when realization struck. Dwight. The word almost left his mouth, but he remembered in the nick of time that he wasn't supposed to know the guy's name. He wanted to turn around. Get a better look. But that would be too obvious.

"Friends of yours?" he asked casually.

"What?" Her eyes darted to him as though she'd forgotten he was there. They were clouded with apprehension and something close to panic. She swiped the hair away from her face with a shaky hand.

What the hell had this jerk done to her?

He turned and sized up both men. Neither one of them was any great shakes in the looks department. Nor in the body department, for that matter. Although it wasn't easy to tell in their preppy tweeds.

The redheaded fellow smiled and waved as soon as he saw Gracie. The other one looked away and made a point of eyeing a short brunette in tight jeans.

Adam felt his temper spark. He knew which one was Dwight. The idiot didn't even have the decency to be civil to Gracie. Adam didn't feel an ounce of sympathy for him. Whatever Zoey dished out, the guy more than deserved.

"Want me to punch him out?" Adam asked, forcing himself to smile and gently touching her hand to get her attention. When her confused gaze found his, he inclined his head in the direction of the two men. "Which one is making you scowl like this?"

The tension dissolved from her face. "Neither," she said, looking surprisingly calm. "They're both old friends." She looked toward the approaching men again, and with a Mona Lisa smile, she murmured, "Just two old friends."

Adam continued to watch her until the men arrived at the table. She no longer looked upset, in fact, she awaited them with a smile. Either she was a damn good actress or she really didn't give a rat's behind.

"Hey, Gracie," the redhead said, giving Adam a quick but genuine smile. "Isn't Zoey here yet?"

"She's behind the counter." Gracie's gaze briefly acknowledged the other man. "Brian and Dwight, this is Adam Knight."

Adam stood.

Brian, the redhead, shook his hand, then waved him to sit down. "I wouldn't give up my seat if I were you," Brian said, glancing around. "Is this place always this packed in the evening?"

Dwight didn't say anything. He didn't even offer to shake Adam's hand, which suited Adam fine. He stood with his hands in his pockets and, through horn-rimmed glasses, eyed Adam's worn work boots.

"The chair's all yours," Adam told Brian. "I was just leaving." He transferred his gaze to Gracie, who was watching him with wary eyes. She looked as though she wanted to say something, but she offered only a wan smile.

"Well, Gracie Klutz, it was nice sitting with you,"

he said, and her grin widened. "I usually don't fall so hard on the first date."

The two men exchanged puzzled glances but she ignored them. "I'm not usually so ticklish."

Dwight coughed.

Adam laughed as he pushed away from the table. "See you Tuesday, Gracie."

Chapter Three

"Has he called or come by yet?"

When Gracie looked up from counting the cash in the register, she saw that Zoey barely had one foot in the boutique. She shook her head. "Stop already. He's not going to come. He was only teasing me. Lock the door behind you."

Zoey did as she was asked then hurried in to lean over the counter and grin goofily at Gracie. "He'll show up. He's hot for you." Something caught her eye in the display case. "Are those new earrings?"

"Get your hands off. I just cleaned that glass. Besides, I've already set aside a pair of purple dangles for you."

"Cool. I'll look at them tomorrow. I want to get to aerobics class early."

Gracie gave her a bland look as she stashed the day's cash and receipts in the floor safe. "Since when?"

Zoey squinted. "You do, too, so don't give me that look. He'll be there."

"No, he won't. You're being silly." Gracie turned her back on her friend and scooped up an armful of clothes to put into inventory. She didn't want Zoey to see any lingering hope in her face. She'd been trying to put Adam's parting words out of her mind all day. Heck, all weekend. Yet a small seed of anticipation had embedded itself in her belly, and no matter how rational she tried to be, it had grown like a darn weed.

She'd had to count the day's receipts three times, and she'd finally given up without balancing. Tomorrow her head would be clearer, she figured. After she proved to herself tonight that men like Adam Knight didn't flirt with dull women like her.

"You're not going to do that now, are you?" Zoey squinted at the assortment of leggings and togas Gracie carried. "Wait a minute," she said, yanking out a magenta toga from the bunch. Next she grabbed a sheer peach-colored one. "You didn't tell me you had a new shipment."

Zoey hurried to the wall mirror and held both togas up to herself, cocking her head at her reflection.

"We didn't," Gracie said. "These are from the last shipment. You have enough clothes."

Zoey stared at her in the mirror, and Gracie averted her face by busying herself with hanging the clothes on the proper racks. She'd known what was coming and she'd felt the heat blossom in her cheeks the minute Zoey had pulled the clothing from her arms.

She never held back on Zoey. Never. One of their favorite pastimes was Zoey modeling all the funky clothes that came through the shop. More often than not, Zoey ended up buying half of them.

"I can't believe you let the other customers get first dibs," Zoey said, the hurt plain in her voice.

"I didn't."

"What were they doing out here, then?"

Gracie sighed. She didn't want to admit that she'd been the one trying them on. Zoey would think she'd really flipped. "They were still in the back until this afternoon, Zoe. Honest." She shrugged. "I'm sorry. I guess I just haven't been myself."

Zoey walked up and patted her arm, a devilish glint lighting her eyes. "You weren't trying them on, were you?" she asked, then burst out laughing.

Gracie rolled her eyes and returned to her chore before her face ended up scarlet. She'd had a problem with blushing since she was a kid. Now, at thirty-two years old, the prospect of growing out of it didn't look too promising.

"Actually, I *was* thinking about hanging my navy blue suits up for some gray ones," Gracie said wryly.

Zoey laughed again. "How risqué of you." She hung the magenta toga on a rack, then stepped back to eye the sheer one she held. "I'm going to take this one. Shall I wait until tomorrow?"

"Take it with you now. We'll write it up in the morning."

"Good." Zoey got a bag from behind the counter and glanced at the wall clock. "Are you ready?"

Gracie grabbed her purse from its hiding place under the register and resisted the urge to check her reflection in the mirror. He wasn't going to be there. And even if he was, it didn't matter. The last thing she was in the market for was another man. She hadn't even gotten rid of all the water rings on the coffee table yet.

By the time they arrived at the other end of the

mall, Gracie had gotten her warm-up. She'd never seen Zoey move so fast. And truthfully, for no good reason, she was anxious, too. Her heart beat too fast, and an odd little flutter in her stomach made her wish she'd skipped the strawberry frozen yogurt after lunch.

As they approached the studio entrance, Gracie saw Haley Morgan and her sister, Heidi, standing outside talking, and a sudden jolt of disappointment threw her entire system another notch off kilter. Adam wasn't here. If he were, Haley would be inside sniffing around.

"Hey, Gracie." Haley threw a paper cup she'd been sipping from into a trash can and trotted to meet them.

"Oh, great," Zoey muttered under her breath. "The barracuda is here tonight."

Gracie bit the inside of her cheek to keep a straight face. "She's not that bad."

"Guess what, Gracie?" The tall leggy blonde's eyes were bright with excitement, and for a moment Gracie felt the flutter in her stomach return. Maybe he was here. "I got the job," Haley said, "I'm going to start teaching step classes on Wednesdays and Thursdays."

"Good for you." Gracie managed a smile. She wasn't disappointed, she told herself. Not in the least. She'd never really expected him to show up. She wasn't sure what she would have said if he had.

"We can choose our own music, can't we?" Haley asked as she fell into step beside them, flexing her arms and shoulders as if she had extra energy to burn. "I don't want to use that old eighties stuff. No offense." She smiled. "I want something young with a lot of zip that'll really get us going."

Gracie and Zoey exchanged private glances, and Zoey rolled her eyes. Haley was only about eight years younger than they were, so why did Gracie suddenly feel like her mother?

"I have to go change," Gracie said, and slinging her bag over her shoulder, she headed for the back of the studio.

"Me, too," Zoey said, and hurried after her despite the fact that she was already wearing her purple leotard.

"Want me to warm everyone up?" Haley called after them. She was still flexing, rotating, moving.

"No, thanks," Gracie said over her shoulder, then murmured to Zoey, "I may have to hurt her."

"Wait your turn."

Gracie grinned. "Feeling a little old?"

"What did you say?" Zoey cupped the back of her ear and cocked her head.

Laughing, Gracie ducked into the locker room. Zoey hesitated near the door, scanning the clusters of women mingling throughout the spacious studio. "Does he know what time class starts?"

"Who?"

"Oh, please." Zoey dropped her bag on the floor near the mirror, then slumped against the wall and slid into a sitting position. "Maybe he'll meet you after aerobics is over and take you to coffee."

Gracie hopped on one foot, trying to pull off her navy slacks. "You're making too much of this."

"He'll be here."

Gracie ignored the confidence in her friend's voice

and concentrated on getting changed. She was a stickler for promptness, and her students counted on classes to begin on time. Besides, she didn't expect or want Adam to be here.

"New leotard?" Zoey asked, squinting at the red and white straps crisscrossing Gracie's bare back.

"No," she lied, and hurried out of the locker room before Zoey saw the telltale blush climbing Gracie's neck.

ANYTHING that could go wrong skipped the meager wrong stage and erupted into disastrous. Adam couldn't remember when a job had been so unpredictable. It didn't help that the construction site was at the tail end of a busy mall and that the cement mixers and supply trucks were often delayed trying to get from one end of the parking lot to the other.

He glanced at his watch. Gracie's aerobics class would be over in ten minutes. If he were smart, he'd stay right where he was and made sure the men finished today's job. The trouble was, he wasn't feeling very smart.

He motioned for his foreman, and after giving the man some instructions, he pulled a flannel shirt out of his truck and slipped it over his T-shirt while he hightailed it to the other end of the mall.

The music was loud with a lot of bass, and it blasted him when he opened the door to the studio. Several women turned to look at him as soon as the door banged shut, but mostly everyone kept jumping or flexing.

As soon as his eyes adjusted to the frenzy of activity and the blur of bright pinks and yellows and blues, he spotted Gracie at the front of the pack.

He stepped to the side, craning his neck for a better look at her.

He wasn't disappointed. Her smile brightened her face like a well-lighted Christmas tree, and he grinned when she suddenly blew stray tendrils of hair off her face. Except her cheeks were moist from exertion, and the wisps clung stubbornly no matter how much she blew.

Stuffing his hands in his pockets, he relaxed against the wall, still smiling.

She didn't see him. Her concentration remained focused on her class, and a couple of times she called out words of encouragement to some of them. And although he wished he could get a better view of her, he preferred his anonymity more.

Within seconds the music changed to a slower beat, and he heard a collective sigh of relief. Then everyone laughed and glanced good-naturedly at each other while they changed positions, some gazes straying his way, and just like that, his anonymity was over.

Pair after pair of eyes turned his way. He pushed off the wall and straightened.

"Ready for cool down?" Gracie called, oblivious to the undercurrent. She turned, giving the class her back, and sweeping one arm out, she arched her body to the side.

She was either naturally graceful or she'd used this routine a long time, because her entire body flowed in harmony with the soft lilting sounds of Mariah Carey.

Adam couldn't take his eyes off her. Automatically he shifted for a better angle.

Her semibare back glistened with a fine sheen of moisture. And the high cut of her red exercise clothes showed off long, killer legs. He'd seen them the other night, of course, bare beneath that denim dress, but he didn't remember having the wind knocked out of him.

A minute later she turned to face the class and stretched her body to one side, her movements slow and sensual. In a voice equally soft and seductive, she called out moves to the class that made Adam's body respond on a level for which he hadn't been prepared. He rammed his hands deeper into his pockets to stretch out his too-tight jeans. There was barely any room to do so, and he groaned silently with the effort.

When she finally straightened, her eyes met his.

She did a double take. She jerked, then grabbed a nearby towel, looped it around her neck and mopped her face.

The class looked a little confused. Some of the women kept up the routine. The majority of them stopped and looked his way.

"Okay, everyone, that's it for today. I'll see you all Thursday." Gracie flashed them a smile and abruptly turned to flip off the music box and fuss with the tape.

Adam took another quick opportunity to check out her legs. And more. He waited for most of the women to wander toward the back of the studio, gritting his teeth through their curious stares.

One tall blonde continued to linger near the boom

box, flipping through a stack of cassettes and frowning.

"Hey, Adam."

Until he heard her voice, he hadn't seen Zoey. She was still sitting on the floor, her face flushed, and not even her neon pink sweatband kept her hair from sticking out in several directions.

"Did you just get here?" Zoey asked, and with great effort struggled to her feet and limped toward him. "Whoever invented exercise needs to be shot."

The blonde turned. Her eyes widened when she saw Adam. And then she smiled and set the cassettes aside. "Now, Zoey, exercise is our friend. If we don't keep moving, gravity will do nasty things to our tushies."

Zoey grimaced and mumbled something about a barracuda. Louder, she said, "Haley, don't you get enough exercise swimming?"

Gracie had turned to face them. Her eyes widened, her gaze flicking from Zoey's deadpan to the younger woman's frown, then she looked down and pressed her lips together.

The blonde's eyebrows drew together. "Swimming?"

Zoey smiled sweetly. "Never mind. So, Adam, you just get here?"

"Just a couple of minutes ago." He looked at Gracie. "I wish I could have made it for the beginning of the workout."

"You do aerobics?" the blonde asked.

He shrugged. "I'd give it a shot."

"I teach a step class starting tomorrow." Haley

pointed a toe and flexed, then adjusted her thong. "At six-fifteen. It's my first one."

"Good luck with it." Adam smiled and turned to Gracie. "What are you doing now?"

Zoey chuckled. "Come on, Haley, I'll help you pick out some music for tomorrow."

"I don't want any of that old stuff," the blonde said as Zoey, scowling, led her toward the back of the studio.

Adam waited until they were safely out of earshot before he said, "I like your moves, Gracie Klutz. Have you been doing this long?"

"It's Allen," she said, grinning. "And you weren't so crazy about my moves Friday night."

"Don't be so sure."

She picked up the end of her towel and dabbed at her face. The makeup she'd been wearing had mostly faded. Her cheeks glowed with the exertion of her workout, and her eyes were bright with it, too. And her smile…well, she had the same great smile he hadn't been able to get out of his mind since Friday evening.

"There's going to be another class in about twenty minutes," she said, and reached for the boom box. He scooped it up first. "You still have time to sign up."

"Are you teaching it?"

"No, but I know the instructor. She's very good."

"I'll pass. Besides…" He grinned and massaged the area of his chest over his heart. "I think I already got a workout."

She frowned, then her gaze drifted toward Haley's disappearing form. "I bet."

"Look, how about a drink or cup of coffee?"

"Not after a workout. Besides, I have to shower."

"I can wait."

"I've got to work tomorrow."

"So do I. It's still early." He saw hesitancy in the way she massaged the back of her neck and he tried not to cringe when he added, "Look, we can even go have carrot juice or whatever it is you drink after a workout."

She wrinkled her nose. "Actually, I usually have a double scoop of jamoca almond fudge."

He laughed. "All right. I'll meet you out front in…what? Fifteen minutes?"

"Maybe we should make it another night."

"Why?" He glanced at his flannel shirt and jeans, and his jaw tightened. His work boots were scuffed, but they weren't dirty. "I'm not dressed right," he said dryly.

"Oh, no," she said quickly. "It's not that. I'm the one who needs an overhaul. And I hate making you wait."

He relaxed. "I don't mind."

"It won't take me long to shower, but my hair." Shrugging, she picked up a thick lock that had escaped her ponytail.

He lifted a hand and rubbed several strands between his fingers. Even after her workout she smelled good. He couldn't identify the fragrance she wore, but it reminded him of cinnamon and cloves and touched something deep inside him. "Your hair looks great."

She blinked and stepped back. "Right."

He dropped his hand. "I'm being presumptuous again."

"No, I'm just not used to—" She stopped and gave him a shaky smile. "Let me go shower." She reached for the boom box. "I'll leave this in my locker."

He nodded and let it go. She got several feet away and turned back to him. "Okay if Zoey comes?"

He shook his head. "I want you to myself."

Gracie stood there, a little stunned. She didn't know what to say. She hadn't expected that answer. In fact, she'd only asked him out of courtesy, or habit, or whatever it was that made her expect that Zoey would automatically be included. When Gracie was with Dwight, Zoey had always been included.

"Well, we normally go home together. She's giving me a ride."

"I'll give you a ride."

"But I don't want to leave her out, either."

"If you two have standing plans, I don't want you to chump her." Adam drummed his fingers against his thigh. "Look, ask her. We'll fly solo the next time."

"Ask her what?" Zoey asked from behind Gracie.

Gracie whirled, startled by her friend's voice. "Adam invited us out for ice cream."

"He did, huh?" Zoey's eyes narrowed on Adam. Her hair was wet and hung thick and black around her pale face. She had to have taken the quickest shower in history. "We can't. Dwight's picking us up at any minute."

"Dwight?" The boom box suddenly felt like a hundred-pound barbell at the end of her arm. "Why?"

"Because I asked him to. I took my car to the shop

at lunch. My transmission was doing something weird again.''

"Zoey," Gracie drawled, the irritation in her voice plain. She darted Adam a look of apology. Zoey knew better than this. Going to the concert with Dwight had been uncomfortable, after all. She didn't know what her friend was up to, but it was going to stop. "We'll talk about this later."

"In the meantime, Dwight's already on his way here." Zoey slid Adam a cool look, which Gracie was totally helpless to understand. Zoey had seemed more concerned that Adam show up than Gracie had. Now she was treating him as if he was unwelcome.

She gritted her teeth. She didn't know what Zoey's problem was, but she was not going to depend on Dwight for a ride home. "I'm going to take a shower now," she said, and gave her friend a significant look. "Don't you want to do your makeup?"

Zoey pursed her lips. "I think I'll just shoot the breeze with Adam while we wait for Dwight. You don't mind company, do you?" she asked him.

"Of course not." Adam lazily looked from Zoey to Gracie. "If you don't mind my borrowing your friend for a couple of hours."

Zoey hesitated, an odd hint of challenge in the lift of her chin. "She's a big girl."

The silence was thick for the next few seconds. Almost as thick as the tension. Gracie stared from one to the other. Something very strange was going on here. First Zoey seemed to be pushing her at Adam, and now she was acting like a mother lion.

"Zoey, you have to start taking cooldowns a little more seriously," Gracie said, shaking her head.

"Getting oxygen to the brain is a good thing." Then she glanced at Adam. "I won't be long."

Zoey blinked, surprise evident in her rising voice. "Are you going with him instead of us?"

Several serious reservations flashed through Gracie's mind, and she hesitated. While she did, the studio door opened, and Dwight popped his head inside.

Gracie was the only one facing him, and she saw that he was wearing her favorite shirt—one she had given him last Christmas. It was a curious thing for him to be wearing, though. He'd never hidden the fact that he didn't like that shirt. An unexpected ache cramped her chest.

It didn't stem from regret or longing or anything readily identifiable. She suddenly felt very empty. As if everything familiar had been ripped away.

She tried for a bland smile. And clearly failed. Because Zoey and Adam, concern on their faces, both turned to see what she was looking at.

Zoey broke into a grin and waved. "Hi, Dwight. Over here."

He sauntered in, slowing down to glance at two women standing near the locker room. The move was calculated and obvious. And when his eyes found hers, with a sudden feeling of exhilaration Gracie realized that she no longer gave a damn about him and his petty attempts at manipulation.

Instead, she felt a little sorry for him and wondered what had shaken his confidence so severely that he had to put her down in order to feel good about himself. And she wondered why she hadn't recognized the insecurity that had undermined their relationship from day one. But he wasn't her problem anymore.

"Hello, Dwight," she said pleasantly as he approached.

He briefly looked at Adam and Zoey but acknowledged neither of them. "Are you ready?" he asked in his typical sullen tone.

"Zoey is," Gracie said, and found it wasn't at all difficult to maintain a smile. "Adam's taking me home."

Chapter Four

She was still in love with him.

Adam should haven't been surprised at that. He certainly shouldn't be concerned. This was merely a job for him. And not even a real one. As soon as he had a moment alone with Zoey, he was going to return the fifty dollars she'd somehow slipped into his pocket.

But there was something about Dwight that irritated the hell out of him, and even though it was none of his business, he knew the guy didn't deserve Gracie. Of course, why Adam thought he knew *that* was another matter altogether. He barely knew her.

"Aren't we going to Spumoni's?" she asked when he'd guided her toward the mall's south exit.

"I thought we'd get out of here. Maybe go for a drive. Isn't there an ice cream parlor near the river?"

Gracie grinned. "I'm not sure if they're still open for business. A lot of the shops around there closed down last year."

Adam did a double take. "What's that smile for?"

"I haven't heard the term ice cream parlor in years."

"Are you implying I'm old?"

"That could be a tricky answer." She paused, amusement continuing to lurk at the corners of her mouth. "Especially since I can't be far behind you. And," she added with a wry lift of her brows, "after Haley insisting on taking the class through the warm-up tonight, I'm feeling a little geriatric myself."

"Haley?"

"The tall blonde."

Recognition dawned. "Oh, the kid with the orange tennis shoes."

Her grin broadened. "Yeah, that *kid*."

"Okay." He half laughed, half groaned. "Now I really sound old. She's not exactly a kid, is she?"

"I just think it's funny that it was her tennis shoes you noticed."

Adam smiled. He'd actually noticed a little more, but he sure as hell wasn't going to point *that* out. Anyway, his answer seemed to please Gracie.

When they got to the parking lot, he ushered her toward the row where he'd parked and indicated when they arrived at his truck. She stopped at the white Mustang beside it and reached for the passenger door.

"Wrong one," he said, and pointed to the large black pickup.

She wrinkled her nose.

Adam pulled out his keys. The truck was clean, inside and out. Hell, it was practically new. He wouldn't have guessed her to be one of those women who judged a man by his set of wheels.

"I didn't know you were from out of town," she said, and immediately hopped into the passenger side. "Weren't those Texas plates I saw?"

Okay, so he'd jumped to a conclusion. "Yup."

"Is that where you're from?"

"I've spent some time there, but I was born in Atlanta."

"You don't have an accent."

He laughed. "I may have had a mild one when I was younger, but I've lived in too many different places since then."

"But you live here now?"

"Nope. Just passing through."

"Oh." Gracie turned to look out the window.

"How about you?"

"I've lived here all my life. In fact, I went to that high school." She craned her neck for a better look as they drove by a rambling three-story brick building. "They still have the same carved wooden mascot out front as when I went there."

He glanced at her. She had a cute profile. "Of course that was only a couple of years ago."

"More like six crow's-feet ago."

"Ah, I see the surgery was successful."

She laughed off the compliment and angled the open side window toward her still damp hair.

"Did we decide where we want to go?" he asked.

"I have ice cream at my house."

The words were spoken softly, hesitantly. Surprised, he swung a look in her direction. But his instant reaction obviously gave her second thoughts, because she started fidgeting with her bag and said, "Maybe that's a bad idea. I only have the low-fat stuff. You might not like it."

"Hey, how do you think I got these abs?" he asked, hoping to reclaim the light mood.

"Yuppie gyms."

"Yeah, that's it. So, are we going in the right direction?"

After a brief pause, she said, "If we're going to my house we are."

"I'm game."

"Adam?"

"Yeah."

"Ice cream is all I have to offer."

"I know that, Gracie." His eyes briefly left the road to rest on her wary face, and he smiled. "That's all I'm asking for."

She nodded and visibly relaxed. "Turn left at the next light."

Within five minutes they were at her house. It was a small two-story light blue Cape Cod nestled in a cul-de-sac. Two gray stone pots were stationed one on either side of her door, filled with red geraniums. Along the front window, white impatiens overflowed from a planter box.

It took her three tries to get the key in the lock while Adam watched uneasily. He wished he could reassure her, tell her that there was nothing to be anxious about, but if he pointed out her nervousness, he would no doubt make matters worse.

Besides, what would he tell her, anyway? He had no idea what he was doing here. This wasn't part of his deal with Zoey. He knew that's why she'd been ticked off earlier. He was supposed to make Dwight jealous. Not have dates alone with Gracie.

She flicked on a switch, and lamps on either side of the light green floral couch painted the cozy living room with a soft glow. A bouquet of fresh flowers sat off center on the square coffee table. He wondered if they were from Dwight.

"Oh, don't take those off," she said when she turned to find him unlacing his boots.

"I'd feel better if I did." He eyed the cream-colored carpeting. "I've been working at a construction site all day."

"Believe me, this place is bulletproof. Dwight used to—" She stopped herself, her fingers fluttering to her throat. "I could really use that ice cream. And something to drink."

Adam pulled off his boots, glad he'd worn new socks today. Usually a hole or two didn't faze him. Especially at six in the morning.

She opened a closet door and dropped her canvas bag inside, then hung her purse on the doorknob. She turned to face him and laced her hands together. She'd be mortified if she knew he'd seen the slight tremble in her fingers.

"You want to have a seat," she said, "while I go rummage through the freezer to see what flavors I have?"

"Unless I can help."

"There's a TV in the corner." She started to gesture to an antique cherry cabinet, then tightly clasped her hands together again. "I think there's a remote somewhere around here."

"Go get the ice cream. I'll entertain myself."

She started to walk toward the back of the house. "You want coffee or a soda?"

"Water would be great," he said, and stopped himself from again asking if she wanted help. What she probably wanted was a few minutes of privacy. He hoped she didn't regret inviting him home.

"Coming up," she said, and hurried off.

He settled onto the couch and picked a magazine off the end table. The publication had to do with investing and financing and contained so many charts it was enough to make anyone's head spin. In the margins on one particular page, someone had penciled in some calculations. He wondered who they belonged to—Gracie or Dwight. Zoey had said Gracie was smart, and Adam didn't doubt that. Although she didn't seem like the pretentious scholarly types he was used to.

He let out a long, exasperated sigh. It was wrong for him to be here. It was wrong for him to be wondering about her at all. He should have just dropped her off. He knew why she'd accepted the ride. Because it had ticked Dwight off. The guy was jealous, and he was having second thoughts about the breakup. Adam had seen it in the menacing gleam in Dwight's eyes. He wondered if Gracie had picked up on it.

Shifting wearily, he yawned and thought again about how he had no business being there. He'd had four killer days in a row with little sleep and numerous roadblocks on the job. Letting his head drop back on the couch, he stared at the faint white-on-white pattern on the ceiling, wondering when he had last been in a real, honest-to-goodness house.

Gracie's muted color scheme was a far cry from the endless orange vinyl motel rooms he'd been renting for the past few years. Although her living room wasn't so perfect that you felt as if you couldn't put your feet up, it was tastefully decorated with just the right amount of homey touches to warm the place.

Feeling comfortable, he slumped a little further into the soft cushions before he flipped to the next page and started browsing an article on how to obtain a small business loan.

GRACIE DUSTED OFF the retired oak tray, then tried to rub out a small dark spot in the corner. It was obviously an old stain, and she finally gave up and placed a yellow linen napkin on the surface.

She waited until she'd loaded the tray with glasses of water and silverware before she dished up two different kinds of ice cream. Her hands had finally quit shaking, and she took a deep, calming breath.

She usually wasn't so jumpy. Except that halfway home she'd realized what a fool she was. After all, Adam was a total stranger. She'd only briefly met him Friday evening. And here she'd invited him into her home.

And then she'd realized that ax murderers didn't offer to take their shoes off.

Smiling, she carried the tray into the living room.

He looked comfortable sprawled on her floral couch, his long legs stretched out in front of him, his head slightly bowed over a magazine lying across his lap. The lamps didn't provide adequate reading light, so she slipped between the sofa and coffee table to set the tray down, then reached over to adjust the lights.

It was an awkward position, wedged between the coffee table and sofa. She'd automatically zeroed in on the only bare spot on the coffee table so she didn't have to move the flowers and expose Dwight's water rings.

But now Adam was in the way, and he didn't seem inclined to move as she tried to reach around him.

She cleared her throat. "I wasn't sure what flavor ice cream you wanted," she said, because she thought maybe he was so engrossed in reading that he hadn't seen her.

When he suddenly jumped, she did, too.

He blinked several times, then stared at her, and she realized he'd dozed off.

"I didn't mean to startle you," she said and backed up. She was close to him. Too close. He squinted, and she lamely pointed to the lamp and said, "I was trying to turn up the light."

She couldn't imagine what he was thinking. She'd practically been on top of him. Even now, the backs of her calves were flush with the adjacent wing chair, and as much as she'd like to disappear between the seams of the carpet, she just stood there, only a couple of feet away, while he studied her with open curiosity.

"I didn't mean to fall asleep," he finally said, then looked at his watch. "How long was I out?"

She shrugged and dropped into the chair. This wasn't where she'd planned on sitting. But she didn't want to hover over him, either. "I was in the kitchen for less than ten minutes."

He drew in his legs and stretched his arms above his head. In this new position, his right knee ended up close to her left one, nearly touching, and she promptly stood again.

He frowned, watching her hurry to the other side of the coffee table and start fussing with the tray.

"I'm sorry about falling asleep," he said. "I don't usually do that on a date."

She nearly flipped a spoon across the room. "I wouldn't consider this a date," she said, and handed him a bowl of vanilla fudge swirl and the temperamental spoon. "And I don't mind that you fell asleep."

She was used to men falling asleep on her, she realized.

He smiled, balanced the bowl on his knee and reached for a glass of water. "Is this mine?"

"Oh, sure. Help yourself."

He took a sip, then held the glass uncertainly while his gaze searched the table. "Have you got a coaster or napkin or something?"

"What?"

"A coaster?"

"Here." Absurdly happy, she reached beneath a stack of nesting tables, then set down two floral lacquered coasters. She picked up the second bowl of ice cream. "I have strawberry, too. I should have asked you which one you prefer."

"I like them both." He peered with interest into her bowl. "Give me a bite."

"Of this?"

His lips curved as his eyes slowly met hers. The blood rushed to her face.

Geez, Gracie Louise. Of course he meant the ice cream.

She shoved the bowl at him.

"No, just a bite." He ducked his head forward and parted his lips.

The spoon suddenly felt like a dumbbell in her hand. The metal clanged against the side of the bowl.

"I don't have any communicative diseases, Gracie," he said, the curve of his lips extending, "and feeding me with your spoon wouldn't be any different than kissing. But if this makes you more comfortable…" He held up his own spoon.

The old Gracie would have taken it. The new Gracie lifted her chin.

She wanted to inhale. Deeply. Without releasing a single fragment of breath. Because she wasn't sure there was enough air in the room to last her the night.

But he was watching her closely, his brown eyes alive with amusement…and a wicked gleam that issued a challenge she had to accept.

Taking a firm grip on her spoon, she dipped it into the strawberry dessert and guided it to his mouth.

His tongue rolled out to accept the ice cream and, mesmerized, she watched him watch her while he tasted it with obvious appreciation.

The portion she'd fed him was much too big, and his tongue swept the corners of his mouth until all remnants of strawberry disappeared. His jaw worked with the effort, and his chin dimpled slightly. It was a good chin. Strong and well-defined. Just like the rest of the man.

And Gracie felt the strange little flutter in her stomach that she'd felt earlier.

Calmly, she pulled back her hand…before it started shaking like a leaf in a windstorm.

"Excellent," he said, leaning back. His shoulders spanned the entire width of the cushion. "This stuff is low-fat, you said?"

She nodded, not trusting herself to speak. Then she tried not to stare, shocked to realize that conservative, sensible Gracie Louise Allen wanted to jump this man's bones.

A nervous giggle bubbled below the surface of her calm facade. "I'll go split the two flavors." She jumped up with her bowl and held out a hand for his.

Except he set his bowl on the table, took her hand and tugged her down beside him. "Relax, Gracie." His thumb stroked the inside of her wrist. "I hate seeing you jump around playing hostess. Next time we'll have to go out someplace."

Next time? She wanted to tell him there wouldn't be one. That him being here was a fluke, a mistake. But he was close again, so close that his breath fanned her cheek, and she could see that the corner of his left eye creased in exactly three crinkles.

And Gracie very much wanted there to be a next time.

"What about your place?" she asked.

Her heart somersaulted and nearly ended up lodged in her throat. Had that really come out of her mouth?

Adam obviously had trouble believing she'd said that, too. His eyes narrowed before going blank, and then he softly cleared his throat.

Appalled at herself, she tried to edge away. "I didn't mean that the way it sounded."

He laughed, keeping a firm hold of her hand. "Shoot."

"Don't, Adam."

He let her go and held up both palms. "I was only teasing, Gracie."

"Your ice cream is melting." She stared at her bowl.

"Is it Dwight?"

Her head shot up. "No. Why would you ask that?"

"Last Friday you said you had a boyfriend. I wondered if the guy was Dwight." He pursed his lips. "I also wondered if you were just trying to get rid of me."

She smiled. "I was trying to get rid of you."

He comically clutched his chest, a wounded look in his eyes. "And me being such a nice guy and all."

"Eat your ice cream." Hers was starting to look pretty soupy, but she spooned some up and tried to eat it in spite of the smile that wouldn't leave her face.

He picked up his bowl, too. "I don't have a place. At least not an apartment or house."

Gracie made a face. She'd just been wondering if she should bring that up again and try to explain what she'd meant. "I wasn't trying to—" She stopped and regarded him quizzically. "Where *do* you live?"

"In a motel." He licked the side of his spoon where a thin stream of chocolate was about to drip.

"Why? Are you waiting for your furniture to arrive?"

"Nope. I don't have any furniture. Two suitcases. That's it. And my truck."

"So you *really* just got into town."

"About two weeks ago."

She didn't know why this surprised her. She didn't know what to think about him. "How did you know about the ice cream shop near the river?"

"I worked a job here a couple of years back."

"Is that what you do?" She shrugged, looking for the right phrase. "Go from job to job?"

He nonchalantly leaned over, spooned up a bit of her strawberry and slid it into his mouth. "You could say that."

"Construction, right?"

"On the nose."

"Do you have a specialty? I mean, are we talking about heavy equipment operation or carpentry or..." She waved a hand in a helpless gesture.

"No specialty," he said.

"So, you're kind of like a jack-of-all-trades?"

"In a manner of speaking."

She sighed loudly. "If you don't want to talk about yourself, just say so."

He grinned at her sudden impatience. "There's not much to tell."

"Are you kidding? You roam around the country from job to job. You get to meet all kinds of different people. You could probably write a book."

He stared intently at her. "You don't think that's a little strange? Being so transient?" He didn't so much as blink. He just sat there, waiting for her response, as if there were a right or wrong answer. Of course there wasn't. So why did she suddenly feel as if she was on the hot seat?

"I think you're very lucky. Most people only dream about being able to do that."

"If that were true, they'd just do it."

Smiling, she shook her head. "No. Most people get roped into mortgages before they're ready, or stay at jobs they don't like because they're too lazy or scared to make a change."

"Are we talking about anyone we know?"

"Not me." She glanced around the room and sighed. "Although sometimes a mortgage can seem overwhelming."

"But you don't think there's anything wrong with a thirty-four-year-old man who hasn't settled down yet?" he asked, still watching her, his eyes curious yet oddly intense. "Someone who'd rather do manual labor than wear a suit all day?"

She laughed, tucking her legs under her and wiggling into a more comfortable position. "Of course not. That's a personal choice."

"Gracie?"

"Hmm?" She scooped up the last of the too-runny ice cream.

"I'd really like to kiss you."

Chapter Five

He shouldn't have asked. Adam knew that by the guarded look on her face. Her eyes had darkened to the point of looking navy, and her brows puckered with indecision.

If he'd simply leaned over and kissed her, she would have let him. And her hands wouldn't have balled into tight little fists, and he wouldn't be feeling like a big heel for pushing her. He knew this as well as he knew that it was time for him to leave.

A vivid curse echoed its way through his brain.

This wasn't like him. He didn't beg for kisses like some damn schoolboy. And he didn't feel so absurdly pleased that someone hadn't judged him.

He set his empty bowl on the tray. "The kitchen is back that way, right?"

"I'll do that." She stood and immediately busied herself with loading the tray.

He drew a hand down his face, covered his mouth for a moment, then stood. "Look, Gracie, I hope what I said doesn't change anything between us."

"It's already forgotten." Straightening, she lifted a

shoulder and smiled brightly. "You look beat. I don't mind if you want to go on home now."

His lips twisted wryly. "That's the nicest way I've ever been thrown out.

Her eyes widened. "I wasn't trying to get rid of you. I wanted to show you there's no hard feelings. Stay as long as you want." She looked so distressed at his misinterpretation that he believed her. "In fact, maybe you should have some coffee before you go. I don't want you falling asleep at the wheel."

This time he wasn't going to be foolish and warn her or ask permission or anything else. He reached over and caught both her hands.

"Come here, Gracie," he said, slowly pulling her toward him. There wasn't much room between the coffee table and the sofa, and it was a little awkward trying to navigate her. But she came willingly, her head tilted back, watching him closely.

As soon as she was a breath away he slid his arms around her and pulled her close, briefly closing his eyes and inhaling the clean scent of her freshly washed hair.

The hug was tentative at first, on both their parts. He hadn't meant to pin her arms down, but she'd been reluctant to slip them around his neck. Either that or she hadn't known what to expect when he'd pulled her to his chest.

But he knew the moment Gracie started feeling safe because she cautiously bracketed his waist, then slid her hands up his back. Her nails lightly dug into his shirt, urging him closer.

He didn't need much encouragement. He snuggled her as close as he could without crushing her, stroking her back, rubbing his chin over the top of her hair. Until there wasn't a spare breath between them, until there was nothing but two ineffective layers of fabric.

And a boyfriend she was still in love with.

Adam breathed deeply, then pulled back.

Gracie couldn't breathe. She could barely move. She'd just very possibly experienced the best hug in recorded history. If there was an award given for hugs, this man would win hands down.

She didn't want him to stop. Ever. But when he pulled back, she did, too.

"That wasn't so bad, was it?" he asked, a lopsided smile lifting one corner of his mouth.

"It felt good." She moistened her lips. "You felt good." And then the heat surged through her face.

"There's nothing wrong with friends hugging, is there?" he asked, ducking his head to meet her eyes, his hands still loosely cupping her hips. "Are we friends, Gracie?"

She had trouble staring into those brown depths. He looked sincere enough, but they couldn't be friends. Not yet. They hardly knew each other. Yet maybe that wasn't so bad, either. Contempt hadn't had time to breed.

She nodded, because it was easier than talking or explaining or having to think. He removed a hand from her hip, and she started to breathe a sigh of relief until he angled her chin up. And then she couldn't breathe at all because, staring into his earnest face, she suddenly realized that it had been a long time since she'd been touched like this. Since someone had actually wanted to touch her. Not just move her out of the way because he was trying to reach a dinner plate in the cabinet.

"What are you thinking, Gracie?"

"That I'd like to be friends," she said, experimentally taking in a little air.

"Me, too." He dropped both his hands. "I'd still like to help with that tray."

"No way." She stepped back, not because she wanted to, but because not to have done so would've been awkward. "You go get some sleep."

Rubbing the back of his neck, he suddenly looked as though his thoughts were miles away. "Aerobics again this Thursday, right?"

She tried not to read anything into that question. Nodding, she maneuvered herself out from between the sofa and coffee table. "Don't forget Haley's step class tomorrow."

Smiling, he headed toward the door. "Right."

He stopped when he got there, his forehead creased in thought, his hand absently massaging the doorknob as if it were a living, breathing thing.

Gracie watched him, fascinated with the way he palmed and kneaded the brass knob. The movements were slow and sure, and to her astonishment, a flash of erotic thought ricocheted through her brain and left her so dizzy she wasn't sure if she wanted to shove him out the door or drag him to the couch.

"Gracie?" he finally said, and forcing herself to breathe, she raised her gaze to his. "Thanks for the ice cream."

GRACIE CLOSED the ledger and took a sip of her cappuccino. She started to pick up a magazine and then set it down again. She was too distracted to concentrate, especially on something as bleak as her current financial status. Nothing short of a miracle was going to improve her bank account.

She straightened her things into a pile and glanced above the coffee bar door at the red wall clock. Zoey was late, as usual. Generally, Gracie didn't mind. She almost counted on her friend's tardiness because it gave Gracie a few minutes to unwind after a long day on her feet. But today it annoyed her. Each time she heard the door open, she looked up expecting…hoping to see Adam.

It was foolish, really. There was no reason to believe he frequented Cup-A-Chinos. She and Zoey practically lived here during breaks and after work, and they had only seen him that one night. Which brought a disturbing thought to mind, one that had plagued her for the two days since she'd last seen him and had snowballed when he hadn't shown up at aerobics last night.

She didn't know a thing about Adam Knight. She didn't know where he worked or at which motel he was living or how long he planned on staying in town. If he never came by or called, she'd never see him again, and that would be that.

The thought depressed her far more than she cared to admit.

The door opened, and Gracie's head shot up.

Darlene, the owner, breezed through the door, juggling a tray and two packages of fast-food carry-out.

"Hey, Gracie, you gonna be around for a few more minutes?" she asked, slowing down as she passed the table.

"I'm waiting for Zoey."

Darlene grinned knowingly and kept walking. "Good. I'll have time to scarf down my dinner. I've got that small business loan information you wanted in the back. I'll be out in ten."

"Thanks, Dee." Gracie sighed and ran a finger down the edge of the ledger. Back to business. That's where she needed to focus her energy.

Instead of being obsessed with jumping Adam Knight's bones.

Her breath caught, and she felt the guilty flush heat her face as she glanced around the room. This admission wasn't a news flash. It had been a recurring thought since Tuesday night, but it never failed to shock her each time it struck.

Having sex on the brain like this wasn't like her. Not like her at all. And she didn't know quite what to do about it. Other than to throw herself into what she should have been focused on in the first place— looking for a way to buy the boutique.

The door opened, and Gracie jumped.

"You're late," she said as Zoey pulled out the opposite chair.

"Of course." Zoey gave her a funny look. "Today was a nightmare. Everyone wanted to be Madonna." She sat and swung her feet onto a spare chair. "Are you and Dwight doing anything tonight?"

"You know the answer to that."

"You're not doing anything with Adam, are you?"

Gracie returned Zoey's frown. "No. Although I don't know why you'd be upset if I did."

"Who said I would be?" Zoey sniffed, then squinted. "That outfit is new, isn't it?"

She plucked at the rust and gold print tunic and thought about denying it. What was the point? Zoey would leap to her own conclusion, anyway. She shrugged. "It was in last week's shipment."

Zoey cocked her head, frowning slightly. "I'm glad you finally broke down and spent some money on yourself," she said. "It seems like all you do is save for the boutique, but isn't that number a little racy for you?"

"Very funny."

"No, I mean, it's a little sheer, isn't it? Dwight would think you went off the deep end."

"I don't give a flying fig about what Dwight thinks."

Zoey's brows shot up, and she stared for nearly a minute. "You really don't, do you?"

"No."

"Well…I think that's good. You shouldn't. I like the blouse." Zoey fidgeted with the neckline of her T-shirt. "What *are* you doing tonight?"

Gracie hesitated, trying to think up something really juicy to shock Zoey out of her neon pink leggings. She sighed. The truth was so boring. "I'm cleaning house."

"Huh?" Zoey managed to look relieved and horrified all at once. "If I'd known you were that desperate I would have bought you a ticket to go see *Grease* with Brain and me."

Gracie laughed, then quickly sobered. "I need to clean. I've got to rent out a room, maybe two."

"Tell me you're kidding."

"I wish I were. If I have to pay the mortgage by myself, I'll be flat broke every month. Plus, I wouldn't be able to put any money toward the boutique."

"Do you have someone in mind?"

"June Watkins. She manages the food court outlets. I heard she was looking for a place."

Zoey shook her head. "She moved in with her astrologer."

"How about Crystal over at the bookstore?"

"She's joining a convent."

"A what?" Gracie set down her cup. "Isn't she about our age?"

"Maybe a couple of years older."

"I can't believe it. I'm stunned."

"It's not a sudden decision." Shrugging, Zoey flagged down the waitress. "She'd been thinking about it for some time."

"A convent." Gracie shook her head. "She's just hitting her sexual peak."

Zoey's foot slid off the spare chair and hit the table, causing the metal legs to wobble and scrape the black tile floor. Everyone turned to stare at the commotion.

Zoey leaned forward. "What did you say?"

Gracie willed the annoying blush not to come. "I was just reading about that," she said defensively, and gestured breezily to the magazine on the table.

Zoey's gaze lowered to the periodical. When her eyes met Gracie's, there was a distinct twinkle in them. "In *Modern Investing*?"

"Not that one." She swept the pile to the side and felt her face burn with unwanted color. But she lowered her voice and asked, "Isn't it about mid-thirties for women?" She shrugged indifferently and added, "Seventeen for a guy."

"I think so. With Brian and me—"

"Zoey." Gracie held up a hand. "Don't tell me more than I want to know."

"You're not telling me *half* of what I want to know."

"I'm just making small talk. My finances are too depressing to think about."

"So you want to talk about sex?" Zoey folded her hands and rested them on the table as though talking to an errant child. "I don't think so."

"Are you implying that I'm repressed?"

She frowned in thought. "That's too strong a word."

Dwight popped into Gracie's head, and a sudden gust of self-doubt caused her to falter. And then she thought about Adam and his perfect rear...his well-rounded biceps...his long, lean fingers, and the entire room heated up. The experience was both consoling and unnerving.

"Forget it, Zoey," she said, angling her wristwatch toward her. "I've got to go."

"I know what your problem is," Zoey said, leaning back in her chair, and Gracie closed her eyes.

She should never have brought up this subject with Zoey. She knew better. If she hadn't had such a darn one-track mind lately, she wouldn't have slipped up.

Now Zoey was going to lecture her about getting involved with Adam. She'd point out that Gracie knew nothing about him and that her reaction to him was probably the result of being on the rebound. Her friend would remind her that she wasn't thinking clearly.

And the upshot was, Zoey would be right. Gracie

opened her eyes and prepared herself for the unvarnished truth.

Zoey was nodding, a faraway look in her eyes. "We need to find you an eighteen-year-old." Her gaze rested on Gracie's appalled expression, and her eyes softened with sympathy. "I know that's a year off the ideal age, but we'd better keep it legal."

ADAM HOPPED into his truck, turned the key in the ignition and watched a pair of taillights disappear from the parking lot. It was getting fairly dark, and most of the men had already deserted the site. They'd been anxious to leave. Although tomorrow was Saturday, they'd be working a full day. Three of the guys with families had asked for Sunday off, and against his better judgment, Adam had granted their requests.

Each day they'd fallen further behind schedule. One problem after another had arisen, and now a cold wind had driven the temperature down five degrees below normal.

Cursing under his breath, he rolled up the window, then cranked up the radio volume. He wondered if maybe he shouldn't have gone for a beer with some of the guys. Even with as little time as he'd spent there, the motel room was getting old. So were the handful of fast-food joints that were doing an admirable job of boosting his cholesterol.

At least one area of his life was under control.

The deal was off with Zoey. And although he hadn't told her yet, he figured she'd gotten the idea when he hadn't shown up at Gracie's aerobics class last night.

The song on the radio changed to hard rock. Cringing, he searched for an oldies station. As soon as the nostalgic sounds of the Lovin' Spoonful filled the cab of his truck, he leaned back and relaxed in his seat.

By the time he'd left Gracie's house on Tuesday, he'd known Zoey's plan wasn't going to work. Technically, of course, it probably would. Unless he missed his guess, Dwight was having exactly the reaction Zoey wanted. But the problem was that Gracie obviously still loved Dwight, and she was confused, maybe feeling a little down, and the last thing she needed was some guy stepping into her old boyfriend's shoes for a few nights.

The thought chafed. Adam gunned the engine. There were only two other cars parked nearby, and he cut out of the parking lot by the most direct route.

He didn't know if it bothered him more that a nice woman like Gracie was wasting herself on a jerk like Dwight, or if it was more personal than that. Because Adam hadn't counted on chemistry getting in the way. But it had. Big-time.

Even now, three nights later, when he thought about touching her, his body tightened. The scent of her freshly washed hair lingered in his mind, and he'd even thought briefly, absurdly, about painting his truck the pink color she'd worn on her toes.

He seriously needed to get a life. As if he didn't have enough problems in the one he already had.

The driver behind him slammed on her horn, and he realized the light had turned green. He pressed on the gas and turned right, keeping an eye out for any new and untried fast-food joints.

If Zoey wanted to continue with her plan, she would have to find someone else. That's all there was to it. Because he was stepping out of the picture. No question about it. He'd tell her on Monday. He'd make a point of staying away from Cup-A-Chinos so he wouldn't run into Gracie. It would be better that way. Then he'd go to Zoey's hair shop and let her know what he'd decided.

He passed several familiar-looking houses, stopped the truck and got out. As soon as he knocked on the door, the porch light came on. A second later, the door opened.

"Adam?"

Gracie's eyes widened in surprised. Her hair was piled in a lopsided style atop her head, and three long tendrils dusted the shoulder of her gray sweatshirt. She blew at them, then smiled.

"Didn't you look out and see who it was before you opened the door?" he asked, frowning.

"Well, no. I was passing by on the way to the basement and I just automatically opened it when I heard the knock." She glanced at the armload of clothes she held, then at him. "Why are you here?"

He rammed his hands into his jeans pockets. "I have no idea."

"Oh. Well, do you want to come in while you figure it out?"

"Okay." He took a few seconds to wipe his boots, trying to decide when he'd become such a damn fool. Hadn't he just been thinking about how contact with Gracie wasn't a good idea?

She stepped aside, but not before glancing down the street.

"Hey, this was a bad idea. It's Friday, and you're

probably expecting company or going out." Adam started to back away.

"Right." Plucking at her sweatshirt, she made a face. "Dressed like this? I was cleaning. You saved me. Now, come in before we both freeze."

It was cold. Several of the houses he'd passed had sheets of cloth draped over their bedding plants. Gracie had covered two of hers. And that was the gist of it. She was a nice suburban lady who worried about her plants freezing and whether she could get her boyfriend back. Adam was just a nomad who couldn't seem to keep his feet planted in one spot.

He shook his head. He should be at his motel room working on alternate strategies to get the mall job done if the weather turned too drastically.

"Is something wrong, Adam?" Gracie lightly touched his arm, sparking a small jolt of awareness, and he moved helplessly toward her.

She backed through the door, and he followed her into her soft pastel living room.

"I don't normally do this," he said, "stop by without calling, but I didn't have your number."

"Really. It's no problem." She dropped the armload of clothes onto a chair and hopelessly smoothed her hair. Several more tendrils drooped around her cheeks. "How about some coffee or hot tea? I might even have some brandy."

"Sure. Anything."

"Why don't you sit down?"

Adam sucked in a breath and remained standing. He shouldn't have come. He still couldn't quite figure out why he had. "I think I'd better take a rain check, after all," he said, rubbing his stubbly jaw.

Her eyes clouded with confusion and maybe even a little hurt.

Damn. "Have you had dinner yet?" he asked.

She nodded. "You haven't?"

"Nah, I'm going to grab something on the way home."

"The motel?"

"Yeah." He looked around. "Well, it was nice seeing you again."

Gracie smiled then pointed to the couch. The same place he'd sat three nights ago. The same place he'd sat when he'd wanted to kiss her so badly that his heart had raced until he thought he was going to have a heart attack.

"Sit," she said.

He transferred his gaze from the couch to her face and peered at her with narrowed eyes. "What?"

"All I have are leftovers, but pot roast is usually better the second night." She dragged her hands down the front of her jeans. "It'll only take a minute to microwave."

Pot roast? His mouth watered. He couldn't remember the last time he'd had real, honest-to-goodness homemade pot roast. "Absolutely not. I didn't come here for you to feed me."

She grinned at him over her shoulder on her way to the kitchen. "While you're eating, maybe you'll figure out why you did come."

Adam didn't sit while he waited. He paced. Until he knew that the length of her area rug was exactly ten squares and the width five. And then he went to find her.

Her back was to him when he entered the small,

tidy yellow kitchen. Coffee dripped into a glass carafe on her left. On her right, a steaming bowl sat on the counter in front of a Minnie Mouse cookie jar. She was humming softly, but he couldn't identify the tune. Staying on key apparently wasn't one of Gracie's strong suits.

He could have watched her all night, standing silently at the door where he had a perfect view of her perfect round backside. But it was her smile he found himself craving.

When she stretched on tiptoes to reach for something in the upper cabinet, he asked, "Can I get that?"

Gracie jumped. She spun around, clutching her chest. "How long have you been there?"

He noticed her mouth right away. There was color there where none had been before. Not much. Just a pale pinkish tint that glistened as her tongue darted out to moisten her lips.

He had to hide a smile, knowing, hoping she'd gone through the trouble for him. But when it suddenly occurred to him that he could kiss all the color off in two seconds flat, it shook him all the way down to his boots, and it wasn't hard to lose the grin altogether.

"I felt useless hanging around the living room." He walked over and brought down the bowl she'd been reaching for. "I don't want you waiting on me."

"Okay." Her hand fluttered toward a table for two near a bay window. "Why don't you set the table?"

"I can eat on my lap."

"No, you won't. No television, either."

He grinned. "Yes, ma'am."

Her eyes rounded briefly, then her face fell. ''I can't believe I just said that.''

Adam nudged her chin up with the tip of his finger. ''Smile, Gracie, you're going to make a fine mother some day.''

Except there was nothing maternal about the look she gave him. Or the way she slid her tongue across her lower lip. And suddenly the room seemed a lot smaller than it had a moment ago.

He dropped his hand, and her brief smile faltered.

''Honestly, you can eat in the living room if you like,'' she said, and quickly turned to slide some rolls out of a toaster oven. ''Could you get the butter out of the fridge?''

''Only if you promise me something.''

She stopped fussing with the rolls and glanced warily at him. ''What's that?''

''Say you'll have dinner with me tomorrow night.''

''Adam, you don't have to do that. Heating some leftovers isn't exactly putting me out.''

''That's not it. As much as I do appreciate all this,'' he said, gesturing to the food. ''I just *want* to have dinner with you. I like your company,'' he added, and smiled.

She smiled back.

And then she burst out crying.

Chapter Six

The last thing Gracie saw before she covered her face and spun around was Adam's look of terrified shock. A moment later, she felt his hands gently cup her shoulders from behind.

"We don't have to go to dinner, Gracie," he said in a soothing yet uncertain voice. "I'll still get the butter out."

She tried to open her mouth to speak, but her breath caught on a giggle. She gasped for another breath, then said, "Onions."

He paused, his fingers still lightly kneading her shoulders. "You want me to get onions *and* butter, or onions instead?"

She sniffed, chuckled. His grip tightened, and when he tried to turn her to toward him, she hurriedly dabbed at her eyes.

As soon as she was facing him, she gave him a watery smile. "No. Onions made me do that. Red ones, anyway. I was cutting them up for a salad right before you came in and I'm afraid I just had a delayed reaction."

He studied her closely, and she wondered if he

knew she was lying. Half lying, anyway. Red onions did have that affect on her, but she hadn't touched one in three weeks, and if he decided he wanted the salad she supposedly made, she might still have some explaining to do.

But she'd had to come up with something. She'd been as shocked as he was that she'd burst into tears. That kind of display was positively unlike her. She never cried. Not even when Gary Snodgrass had publicly dumped her for Melanie Brown in the tenth grade. Her eyes didn't even get moist when she got two Bs in college and ruined her perfect A record. She was always the rock-solid shoulder for her friends. But Gracie Allen never cried.

"I'm sorry," she said, shrugging. "I hope I didn't upset you."

He brushed a tear from her cheek with the pad of his thumb. "I think maybe it's the other way around."

His touch was so soft, so gentle, and he was so very close that her senses scrambled for balance, and it took her a moment to process what he was saying. "No, it was the onions. Really."

One side of his mouth lifted, and she couldn't tell if he believed her or not. "Now I really am going to upset you."

She dashed away the last of the moisture from her face and, waiting expectantly, stared into his warm brown eyes.

"I don't like onions."

She sniffed. "Me, neither."

They both laughed.

"Dwight always—" She stopped herself. She

could tell by the annoyed look in Adam's eyes that Dwight was not the preferred topic of conversation. Not that she wanted to think or talk about him, either. After all, he'd indirectly been the cause of her distress. Gracie wasn't used to a man wanting her company. Dwight had made it painfully clear that he hadn't.

"Let's sit down," she said. "I'll have some ice cream while you eat your pot roast."

Adam nodded, but she caught his grin as he started to turn toward the refrigerator. She grabbed a handful of his shirt to stop him. "What's the smirk for?"

Laughing, he came to a halt and faced her again. "Do you own stock in some ice cream company or is this just a mild addiction?"

"Hey, I work out. I can afford a scoop now and again."

He looped an arm around her waist and pulled her toward him for a quick kiss on the cheek, his hand lightly stroking the curve of her hip. "Yes, you can, Gracie," he said, grinning, "yes, you can." Just as quickly he released her, went to open the refrigerator door and bent to peer inside. "You want anything else while I'm in here?"

She rubbed the side of her face. It was still warm from his lips. Although his action had been merely friendly, at least nothing more intimate than something Brian would initiate, her skin tingled, and her blood sizzled. "No," she said. "Just go to the table."

Her voice came out a little sharper than she'd intended, and he looked over his shoulder at her. Abruptly she turned to get the rolls. "Unless you want something other than coffee to drink,'' she added.

"A double shot of bourbon.''

She blinked.

"Coffee is fine,'' he said, placing a tray of butter on the table. "Can I pour you some, too?''

"I like the bourbon idea.''

He smiled, and after searching three cabinets, set two mugs on the counter. "Black?''

"Just sugar.''

He carried their coffee to the table while she stuck the pot roast into the microwave for a quick zap. The food had cooled in the past few minutes, although how that had happened she was at a loss to understand. The temperature in the small kitchen had risen by at least ten degrees. Each time Adam carried something else to the table, he seemed to make an effort to brush a different part of her body. It wasn't obvious, and it was probably unintentional. But by the time the table was set and they were ready to sit down, Gracie thought she was going to need a cold compress just to get through the meal.

She settled for rocky road ice cream. Two gigantic scoops of it. When Adam eyed the large bowl with amusement, she ignored him, and for a while they ate in silence.

"This is probably the best pot roast I've ever had,'' Adam said after he'd forked the last chunk of meat.

"You don't have to be polite. I'll still let you have seconds.''

"I'm not being polite. This is great stuff, especially after a week of cheeseburgers and tacos.''

"Ah.'' Gracie nodded as Adam left the table to

dish up another serving. "The pot roast wins by default."

"No, ma'am. I don't even make it this well, and I'm a pretty fair cook myself."

"You?" She watched him study the microwave for a moment, then accurately punch the buttons.

"Sure." He swung toward her and leaned against the counter while he waited for his food to heat. "I did most of the cooking when I was at home."

"Where was your mother?"

Adam grinned. "Now, Gracie, what kind of chauvinistic question is that?"

"I'm a throwback. Sue me."

His grin broadened. "She's a college professor. Most of the time after she was done with her classes she either had lectures to give or faculty meetings to prepare for. Anyway, if my sister or I didn't cook something for dinner, we'd end up eating at ten." He shrugged. "So we learned to cook."

"But you don't do it anymore."

"Tough to do in a motel room."

"Good point."

The microwave dinged, and he withdrew the bowl. Letting out a short yowl, he slid it onto the counter. "Hot."

"There's a pot holder in the top drawer."

"I got it." Yanking the hem of his T-shirt from his jeans, he used it to grab the bowl, then headed for the table.

Gracie got a clear shot of lean tanned skin and a smattering of dark hair. She'd already felt how taut and well-defined his abs were, but getting that unexpected glimpse gave her a serious hot flash.

Her hand was cool from cradling the bowl of ice cream, and she pressed her fingertips to her left temple. *For goodness sakes, it's only a stomach,* she told herself. She stole another quick peek, then averted her eyes and inhaled the rest of her rocky road.

She was going to have to do something about this ridiculous obsession. How was she supposed to have a decent conversation with the man?

Adam lowered his plate onto the place mat, then reclaimed his seat, leaving his shirt untucked.

"Tell me more about your family," she said to get her mind off areas she had no business thinking about.

"Like what?"

"You know…the usual. Like where they live, what the rest of them do." She liked the way his jaw worked when he chewed. It was square and strong, and it probably made him look a little too stubborn, but she liked it. "How many nieces or nephews you have, that sort of thing."

"They all live in Texas, and they all work for universities. One nephew, no nieces."

She laughed when he returned his attention to his dinner as though he clearly thought he'd relayed enough information. "That's it?"

"What?" He stopped chewing and drew his dark brows together, and she found she liked the way he did that, too.

"You want some more coffee?" she asked.

"Maybe after we move those boxes."

"What boxes?"

"The ones stacked up in the foyer. You're moving them down to the basement, aren't you?"

"Eventually. But you don't have to help me with that."

"Why eventually? Let's do it tonight while you've got all this lean, powerful muscle at your disposal." He tried to keep a straight face, she could tell, but the corners of his eyes began to crinkle.

She feigned surprise. "Where?"

He polished off the last bite and swiped a napkin across his mouth, and with mock disbelief, his gaze met hers. "*Where,* you ask?"

Laughing, she picked up her bowl and carried it to the sink. It wasn't the wisest move. She found that her legs and hands were a little shaky, and as she leaned over to open the dishwasher, she sneaked a peek to see what he was up to.

He threw down his napkin and pushed back from the table. His movements were slow, calculated, and, with a combination of dread and excitement, Gracie watched him amble toward her.

She straightened as he got closer. When he laid a warm hand on hers, her pulse nearly leaped through her ratty gray sweatshirt.

"Don't close that yet," he said, his hand leaving hers, then he rinsed his dish before placing it in the dishwasher next to hers.

She let out a breath. This was getting ridiculous. She was as jumpy as a teenage girl waiting by the phone for a boy to call. The next thing she knew she'd be writing to Dr. Ruth.

Stifling a disgusted sigh, she threw their silverware into the dishwasher and shut the door. Oblivious to her, Adam whistled as he continued to clear the table, then stacked their linen napkins and place mats near the sink.

She turned to wipe off the counter, eyed the half pot of coffee and wondered if she should make another. He did say he'd have some later, so she should probably have it ready. On the other hand, if she made it now, it would look like she expected him to stay....

She was hopeless.

Gracie grabbed the sponge and furiously scrubbed the counter. She was going to have a serious talk with herself as soon as he left. Thank goodness her poor unsuspecting guest didn't have a clue she'd turned into some sex-crazed almost middle-aged spinster with one thing on her brain.

Taking a deep breath, she dropped the sponge in the sink, pasted a benign smile on her face and turned.

Her poor unsuspecting guest slipped an arm around her waist and hauled her body against his.

His breath fanned her cheek as his lips stretched across even white teeth. She stared at him, shocked...excited...dizzy, and her breath couldn't seem to make it past her lungs.

"Thanks for dinner, Gracie," he said, his gaze dropping to her mouth. When his eyes raised to meet hers again, his hold slackened a little. "A friendly hug is okay, right?"

She nodded, bringing her hands up to rest on his chest, half afraid her knees wouldn't hold her. He clearly accepted this as some kind of signal because he put his other arm around her and hugged her tight.

Her palms automatically slid up to join in a traitorous pact around his neck, and breathing was no longer a problem. A surge of air rushed from her diaphragm, and in her panic to exhale, her breasts were thrust against him.

He made a noise low in his throat, a moan, maybe, and then he hugged her impossibly close, his hand stroking her back, urging her closer still.

With sudden, staggering clarity, she remembered she wasn't wearing a bra.

Heat burned through her like wildfire.

Her nipples beaded against the fleecy sweatshirt, and an unbelievable ache settled between her thighs. She felt hot and cold all at once and a little wicked, too. She closed her eyes, struggling to grasp what was happening to her.

Surely she was too young for menopause.

So why was she falling to pieces over a simple, friendly hug? Why was she suddenly so hot to trot she was ready to say yes before he even asked?

She opened her eyes and ducked her head so that she didn't have to look at him. But when his roughened chin grazed her temple, her knees got all wobbly again and she had to either pull away or hang on to him.

She pulled away and leaned against the counter.

This was a friendly hug. *He* thought it was. He wasn't getting all hot and bothered. He barely had any expression on his face at all.

While here she was feeling like some damn hot tamale.

She took a deep breath and straightened her spine. She could handle this. Be blasé, worldly. Smiling breezily, with a casual shrug of one shoulder, she said, "All that for some hot tamale." She stopped, mortified. "Pot roast. I meant pot roast."

He laughed.

Oh, God, she wanted to die. Right now. She didn't care if they ever found her body. Because if they didn't, there would be no eulogy and the whole world wouldn't have to know what a big idiot she was.

"See, I was thinking about making tamales tomorrow." She laughed, too, and waved an indifferent hand. "And it just slipped out."

"You know how to make tamales?"

"Of course." She didn't have a clue.

"I haven't had those since Texas."

Oh, God. "Coffee?"

He blinked. "I thought we were going to move the boxes first."

"Oh, those." She started to take his arm, and his elbow brushed her left breast. She shifted away. "Let's go into the living room."

He didn't move. His eyes narrowing, he peered closely at her. "Are you okay?"

She nodded first, then shook her head. "I think I'm coming down with something."

His expression softened. "Poor baby." He slid an arm around her shoulders and guided her toward the living room. "Maybe we should tuck you in bed."

"Oh, no. No, bed would not be a good thing right now." She flashed a brief smile at his puzzled look and started to slip away. "I have too much to do."

He didn't let her go. He caught her fingers and tugged until she stopped, then pressed the back of his hand to her forehead. "You do feel a little warm."

"Really?" She cleared her throat to cover her dry tone and ducked her head. "Probably just allergies. I seem to have uncovered some dust pockets."

She watched him glance curiously around the room. Near the basement door sat four large boxes, a black pole lamp and two folded director's chairs.

"Spring cleaning?" he asked.

"Not exactly. I'm clearing out an upstairs room."

"Are you moving?"

"I hope not." She sat on the wing chair at the same time he sat on the couch and carefully angled her knees away from his. "I'm getting a roommate."

"Zoey?"

"Oh, heavens, no. I love her like a sister, but she'd drive me crazy after a week. Besides, she's married."

"Yeah." He shrugged. "But you never know..."

She grinned. "You do with Zoey and Brian. They'll be married forever."

"Forever is a long time."

"It can be." She cocked her head. "Have you ever been married?"

"Me?" His mouth curved in a mocking grin. "I'd have to stay in one place for that."

"Not necessarily."

He gave her a funny look. "You're an interesting person, Gracie Allen."

"You've got the wrong Gracie," she said in a teasing tone, but he frowned, making her regret the impulsive remark that could so easily be mistaken for self-pity. She braced herself for his admonishment.

His frown dissolved into a thoughtful expression. "Are you sure you don't want me to tuck you in?"

The question took her off guard, and she felt her face flood with color. Shaking her head, she buried her fists into the hem of her sweatshirt, stretching the fabric away from her breasts. Although she had to admit he hadn't given any indication that he knew she was braless. In fact, he hadn't so much as given her chest one wayward glance.

"Okay. Then how about some of that free labor I offered?"

"Really, you don't—"

Adam got up and opened the basement door, then hoisted one of the boxes onto his left shoulder. He grabbed the pole lamp with his free hand. "Any place in particular?"

She scrambled to get ahead of him, turned on the basement light, then grabbed one of the director's chairs. "Follow me."

"My pleasure," he said, and when she shot him a look over her shoulder he merely smiled.

The basement was partially finished. One half had been carpeted in a neutral grayish tan, and dark wood paneling covered two walls. Dwight had started the project. He'd wanted to make one corner an office. Except he never worked at home—he usually played with his computer. Gracie figured his interest in the downstairs office had more to do with putting distance between them.

She turned right after leaving the stairs, taking them through the semifinished half, flipping on lights as she walked the length of the room until she got to the treadmill she had set up in the corner. She pointed to a spot and lowered the director's chair to lean against the wall. "You can dump everything here."

He set down the pole lamp and frowned. "You'll only have to move it again."

"Why would I do that?"

He inclined his head toward the corner where the

two paneled walls met. "You're in the middle of finishing the room."

She shook her head and tried to reach for the box on his shoulder. "Not anymore. Here will be fine."

Adam moved out of her way and set the box down himself. Still frowning, he walked to one of the walls and knocked on it. "Why?"

For a moment Gracie considered deliberately misunderstanding him. She really didn't want to get into this conversation. Or any one that remotely involved her ex-fiancé. She shrugged. "Dwight wanted to do this. Not me."

He bent to check the baseboards. "It'll improve the value of your house. Ever have any flooding?"

"Not since I've been here."

Continuing to pat the walls, he traveled toward the stairs. Then he stopped and knocked on the wood again. "There's a fireplace directly above. It wouldn't take much to build another one here."

"Look, Adam, you're probably a very good—" she shrugged helplessly "—handyman. But I really can't afford—"

A peculiar grin twisted his mouth. "Relax, Gracie, I'm not trying to drum up business for myself."

"No, of course not." She twisted the hem of her sweatshirt. Something in his face, in his tone made her uneasy, like she'd committed some big faux pas. Maybe he didn't like being referred to as a handyman? But wasn't that what he said he did...odd jobs? "Are you ready for some more coffee now?"

His gaze flickered to her face, and she realized he'd been looking at her chest. She promptly released the sweatshirt. It was cold down here, and she could feel her nipples standing at attention. She didn't dare look.

"In a minute." He hit the wall one last time with the heel of his hand. "What's on the other side?" he asked, gesturing in the direction of the stairs.

"Just the laundry room."

"Mind if I have a look?"

Lifting a shoulder, she motioned him in that direction. "Be my guest. But there's nothing to see. It's not finished. There's only ugly brown and tan floor tile and white plaster walls, or whatever that stuff is."

Her description was met with a lopsided grin. "Where's the light?"

She reached past him, her shoulder brushing his, the clean scent of peppermint wafting down to her, and flipped on the switch.

Immediately the long, bare fluorescent bulb sparked to life, sputtered a moment, then flooded the room with light.

"Does it always do that?" Adam asked, frowning.

She nodded and stepped over the threshold where new carpet met worn, drab, ink-splattered tile. "I tried changing the bulb. But apparently that isn't the problem. It always ends up coming on, though." She smiled and turned to look at the room.

Her lips froze. She tried to swallow, but her throat had suddenly grown dry. She'd been wrong when she told Adam there was nothing to see. She'd forgotten about the laundry she'd hung out only an hour before he arrived.

In the corner, over her innocuous white washing

machine, hung a red teddy, black lacy garters, a sheer peach negligee and two pairs of crotchless panties.

She took a deep breath. And dived for the light switch.

Chapter Seven

When Gracie tripped in her haste to shut off the light, Adam caught her. He circled an arm around her waist, bringing her to his side…and two hairs short of reaching the light switch.

"Whoa. What's wrong? Did you think the light was going to go off again?" He frowned at the fluorescent bulb. "I'll have to have a look at that."

Gracie stayed where she was, her body pressed against his, his hand molding the curve of her hip. She stared dazedly at the shadow on his cheek cast by his long dark lashes. And for a moment, she forgot that she had to get him the hell out of here.

Straightening, she said, "That would be great. You checking the light out, I mean." His back was partially to her lingerie, and she took his hand and tried to draw him to the other side of the basement. "Maybe we ought to just leave it alone until you have time."

Without budging, he squeezed her hand, then released it. "I'll look at it now. No sense asking for trouble."

"No, really. You didn't come here to do my chores. Let's go upstairs and—"

He wasn't listening to her. He'd turned toward the light and was staring into the room. She followed his gaze and cringed. The light wasn't quite as good over the clothesline and washer, and the best she could hope for was that he wouldn't be able to tell the panties were crotchless.

He swung a bemused look at her. "You already found a roommate?"

She blinked. "No. Why?"

His gaze strayed to the lingerie for a couple of seconds before he squinted at the light bulb. "Do you have a chair that I can stand on?"

Gracie stared at his profile as he focused his attention on the fluorescent bulb. He didn't need a chair to reach the light. He was tall enough. And when she realized he was trying much too hard to concentrate, comprehension promptly dawned.

He'd initially thought the lingerie didn't belong to her.

She started to smile but reality sneaked in and stole her common sense. Indignant outrage wiped out every reasonable thought.

He figured she was too boring to wear lingerie like that.

Maybe the old Gracie was uninspired, but the new one wasn't. She'd bought the items because of Dwight, because she thought they might spark the old flame. She'd felt foolish and pathetic wearing them. The crowning touch was that Dwight thought she *looked* foolish and pathetic wearing them. But now, wearing these things had nothing to do with Dwight.

She liked them, and she wasn't going to apologize for it. Well, maybe except for the crotchless panties.

"Gracie? The chair?"

Quickly she searched the storage closet under the stairs and noisily dragged out a chrome stool with a torn blue vinyl seat. She pushed it toward him, then put her hands on her hips. "Why did you think I had a roommate?"

He shrugged and took a long time to adjust the stool beneath the light. "No reason."

Let it drop, Gracie. You don't want to get into this conversation. "Was it the lingerie?"

"What lingerie?" He climbed on the stool and began fiddling with the light.

Watching him prod the light without even a passing glance in her direction, she inhaled deeply. She should have been furious that he was ignoring her, but instead common sense started making a welcome return, and her irritation ebbed. It was time to let the subject drop. Nothing could be gained from this discussion. Embarrassment was bound to be the only result. She already felt the heat crawling up her neck. She let her hands drop to her sides.

Adam grunted something between exasperation and resignation and hopped off the stool. "You're right. I'm too old to be game playing," he said, facing her. "I did see that stuff, and I did think it belonged to someone else."

She nodded, feeling a little numb, a little depressed. It didn't matter what Adam thought, she told herself. It didn't matter what Dwight thought. She was no femme fatale. She'd never wanted to be. If she dressed for other people, she would have given up the dull navy suits years ago. What did unnerve her was that she was more fragile than she realized. She wanted to believe that her breakup with Dwight had left her unscathed. Instead, she felt vulnerable, confused and unattractive.

Adam tucked a finger under her chin and raised her face to his. "Would you pay attention here? I'm trying to be really honest, damn it."

She blinked under the intensity of his dark eyes so close to her own, and a short nervous laugh made it past her lips. She'd asked for this. She really had.

As soon as he was assured of her attention, his hand slipped to her shoulder. "Like I said, I did think that maybe those things belonged to someone else, at first. Which of course is ridiculous, and I don't know if that was a defense mechanism, or what. But as soon as I admitted they belonged to you, my mind went haywire." His mouth twisted wryly. "Not to mention a few other things."

Gracie stared, blinked, stared some more. "I'm not sure of what's happening here."

"Geez, Gracie, I had a couple of, uh, impure thoughts, okay?" Shaking his head, he stepped back.

"Impure thoughts?" She tried not to smile. "Really?"

"It won't happen again."

She cleared her throat and pushed back the giddiness threatening to bubble to the surface. "Of course not. You want that coffee now?"

Frowning, he shook his head. "Your light's okay. I think I'd better hit the road."

"WHAT WERE YOU doing at Gracie's last night?" Zoey stomped through the door of the coffee bar, making Adam back up.

In another five seconds he would have been out of here. He'd thought twice about stopping to pick up some coffee this morning. Obviously he should have given it a third thought.

"If you want to talk you'll have to walk with me," he said, sidestepping her and continuing out the door.

"Why are you trying to lose me? A guilty conscience, maybe?" She'd done an abrupt about-face and was right behind him.

"Nope. I have a lot of work to do today." He wondered what Zoey thought he should feel guilty about. Surely Gracie hadn't told her about the lingerie incident. He didn't slow down to find out, though. He figured Zoey was going to tell him whether he wanted to know or not, so he kept a brisk pace down the mall.

It hadn't opened yet, and only a few workers lingered outside the retail shops, checking display windows, unlocking cage doors. Gracie's store was on the opposite side, and he was half tempted to turn to see if he could get a glimpse of her. He kept walking.

"You're not doing this right," Zoey said, taking an extra hop to keep up with him. "You're only supposed to schmooze her in front of Dwight. But he wasn't there, was he?"

"Gee, I really missed him."

"Okay, Adam, if you can't play by the rules, the deal is off. You're fired. Consider this severance pay."

He came to a halt and faced her, ignoring the bills she shoved at him. He'd forgotten about the money she'd slipped him that first day. She wasn't prepared for his abrupt stop, and she nearly collided with a large planter of yellow mums. She straightened and adjusted her oversize T-shirt. Today it read, How Many Roads Must a Man Travel Down Before He Admits He's Lost?

"Okay," he said, reaching into his pocket for a fifty.

"Okay?" Zoey's eyebrows shot up to disappear in her shaggy bangs. "That means you won't see her anymore, right?"

"Wrong."

"How could you come between her and Dwight like this?"

Adam's smugness sank faster than a windless kite, and he floundered for a moment. "There's nothing left between them, Zoey, no matter how much you want there to be."

"Or how much you don't." She shot the words back, and he felt the jab in his midsection.

He tried to pass her the crumpled bill.

"Hit a nerve, did I?" She sniffed in satisfaction as she backed away from him and the money.

"Don't you have hair to fry or something?"

"I have never screwed up a perm in my life." She let out a low growl. "How about if I spill it that you're only kissing up because I'm paying you? Imagine how happy Gracie would be to find out you're nothing but a gigolo."

He held onto his temper with his last shred of control. He didn't want Zoey to see how much she'd gotten to him with that remark. Although it wasn't true, lately he'd been wondering how to tell Gracie about him and Zoey and their defunct deal.

"You won't," he finally said. "I didn't take your money. You sneaked it into my pocket. Besides, you wouldn't exactly come out smelling like a rose, would you?"

She scowled, and he knew he had her. "What about dinner tonight?" she asked. "I'll give you double what I said I'd pay you if you cancel out."

He'd forgotten about dinner. Although he had asked Gracie, they never settled on a time or anything. "What did she tell you about tonight?"

Zoey glowered at him. "Quit testing me. She tells me everything."

He'd bet differently. "Look, Zoey, we're only friends. Did Gracie tell you that?"

Her eyes narrowed. "Then why is she acting weird?"

"Is she?" Adam started to smile, then elation slid into apprehension. What if he was wrong about Dwight? What if he was getting involved in a rebound situation?

The thing was, he had no business getting involved at all. Gracie was a nice person. But he was going to be gone in a couple of months. He could tell her they were just friends until he was blue in the face, but the blood pumping elsewhere made him a liar. Just hugging her made him feel as if he was seventeen again, with all the raging hormones that went along with it. And seeing the lingerie…well, that had been the final straw. His body tightened just thinking about the red teddy.

Maybe Zoey was right. Maybe he had no business

interfering in Gracie's possible reconciliation with Dwight. He didn't like the sight of the guy, and he didn't have to live with him. But Gracie might.

He exhaled a large breath he'd had no idea he'd been holding. He needed a time-out, some space to think.

"Hey, Adam, are you with me here?" Zoey waved the handful of bills in front of his face. "The silent treatment doesn't work with me, buddy."

He met her gaze with a start, and a sardonic grin turned up the corners of his mouth. He didn't doubt her for a minute. "You can quit worrying about dinner," he told her, and pressed his fifty into her free hand. "I'm calling Gracie at lunch to cancel."

SHE HAD at least a dozen errands to squeeze into the next seven hours, and the last place Gracie wanted to be on her day off was at the mall. Mondays always seemed to arrive slowly yet fly by quickly, and this one was even worse because she had made three appointments with three potential housemates who worked there. As much as she'd like to ignore the situation, her finances wouldn't let her.

It had really killed her to write the mortgage check last night. Zoey had urged her to ask Dwight for half of it, but Gracie would have sooner crawled naked on her belly down the center of the mall at noon.

The mortgage wasn't the only reason for her funk, though. She wondered about Adam. She hadn't been in the store when he called on Saturday. Her assistant had given her the message. Gracie almost wished he hadn't canceled, that he hadn't called at all, because then she could have rationalized that they'd never really had a firm date. Now, she had to wonder what had spooked him.

In fact, she wondered if he were even still in town. Since all he did was odd jobs, it was possible that he'd finished up and left. Twice she'd thought about walking past the job site. But that would have been too obvious. And juvenile.

"Hey, kiddo." Zoey appeared from the back of the salon and stopped briefly to glance at her appointment book before coming to sit next to Gracie in the waiting area. As soon as she sat she picked up Gracie's hand and inspected her nails. "My next appointment canceled, if you want a manicure."

"I'd rather go have a cup of coffee. No, make that a stiff drink."

Zoey grinned sympathetically. "You didn't find anyone yet, huh? How many more people do you have to talk to?"

"One."

"What happened to the other two?"

"Missy from the sporting goods store needs enough room for an entire gym, it seems. And Karen over at the cookie shop wants her pet boa constrictor to have full run of my basement." She shuddered thinking about the picture of the little darling that the woman insisted on showing her.

Zoey laughed. "That makes the two you talked with yesterday look a little better."

"Not better enough.

Zoey shrugged. "I keep telling you, what you need is an eighteen-year-old—"

"Can you go for coffee or not?"

"Snappy, aren't we? What else is bugging you?"

Gracie hesitated. "Have you seen Adam?"

Her friend's face fell. "Why?"

"What's the long face for? I though you'd be happy about me taking an interest in someone."

"You *are* interested?"

Gracie rolled her eyes. If her friend were any less enthusiastic, she'd have to jump-start her. "Possibly."

"I know. I'll tell Brian to call Dwight, and we'll all go out to dinner tonight."

Shaking her head, she stood. "You can have coffee with me now, or else I'll see you tomorrow."

Zoey's shoulders sagged. She looked as if she was about to argue, then thought better of it. "Let me get my purse."

"Never mind, my treat," Gracie said as she made her way to the door.

"You can't afford it." Zoey gave her a teasing look before disappearing in the back.

Although she knew her friend didn't mean anything by it and there was only one other person sitting in the corner, the comment stung, and Gracie casually looked around to see if the woman had heard.

Adam stood in the doorway.

She blinked. He was still there, less than four feet away, in jeans and a white T-shirt that was tight from so many washings. His arms and face were tanned despite the cool weather they'd been having, and his nearly black hair was slightly windblown.

"Hi," she said, not sure if she were more disconcerted that he might have heard or that he was there at all. Was he coming to see Zoey?

"Hello, Gracie. I thought today was your day off."

She frowned. So he had come to see Zoey. "It is. I had to talk to some people."

"About sharing the house?" His eyes were sympathetic, and she no longer had any doubt that he'd heard Zoey's last remark.

Well, how embarrassing was this? Maybe if she stuck around the day could get worse. She shrugged and stepped aside so he could get out of the doorway. "Among other things."

"Find anyone yet?"

She sighed. "Only a snake named Fred."

Fleeting panic darkened Adam's eyes. "You wouldn't take in some strange man, would you?"

She chuckled in spite of herself. "*You're* the only strange man I know."

One side of his mouth hiked up. "Is that an offer?"

Her heart thudded. Adam and her...in the same house? "I'm sorry I didn't get to talk to you Saturday." The words rushed out of her mouth before she could stop them and, yes, she found that the day could get worse.

"Yeah." He flexed a shoulder. "Me, too. Work got crazy, and I couldn't call back. I hope I didn't put you out too much."

"Oh, no." She waved a hand. "I had a lot to do."

He seemed to relax a little. "Did you end up making those tamales?"

"What tamales?" Zoey appeared out of nowhere and positioned herself between them. "When did you learn how to make tamales?"

Gracie gave her friend a little shove toward the door and smiled at Adam. "We were just about to go have coffee. Want to come along?"

He briefly glanced at Zoey. "Another time. Maybe I'll see you at aerobics tomorrow."

"Sure," Gracie said, swallowing her disappointment.

"Yeah," Zoey added, "wear your spandex pants."

Adam had started to leave, but he very calmly lifted one brow and asked, "Did Gracie tell you how much she liked my blue ones?"

As soon as Gracie got over the shock of the un-flappable Zoey's stunned look, she burst out laughing.

ADAM HAD obviously been working outdoors too long. His brain had fried in the summer, freeze-dried in the winter. There was no other accounting for what he was about to do.

He waited until the last woman had disappeared into the locker room, then he waved to Gracie from the door of the aerobics studio. If she had seen him earlier, she showed no sign. She pulled the towel from around her neck and waved back. Even though he was several dozen yards away, the brilliance of her smile warmed him.

Keeping an eye out for Zoey, he strode toward Gracie. As best as he could tell, Zoey hadn't been a part of the class, but he didn't want to take any chances on talking to Gracie in front of her. He didn't need Zoey's hostility mucking things up. He'd deal with that later. He wished he could have had his talk with her yesterday, but Gracie's appearance at her salon had taken him by surprise.

"Why do you always show up *after* class is over?" Gracie grinned as he approached.

"Ice cream is just as important as exercise."

Her smile faltered. "Not tonight."

"But they have the best hot fudge in all of Ohio right around the corner."

"You're an evil man." She picked up the boom box and headed for the locker room, and Adam had the sudden sinking feeling that she was blowing him off.

"Are you upset about Saturday?" he asked, keeping step with her.

She looked at him in surprise. "Of course not. Why would you say that?"

He shrugged. "You just aren't interested in ice cream, then."

She looked at him as though he'd committed the worst blunder in history. "I'm always interested in ice cream. But I have two appointments tonight."

"The housemate thing again?" And before she could answer, he added, "I wanted to talk to you about that."

A look of alarm crossed her face. "Such as?"

He frowned. She couldn't know what he was going to say. "After your shower, would you spare me a few minutes? I don't want to discuss this standing here."

They'd reached the locker room entrance and stopped. When she looked at him, her eyes were gleaming with suspicion. "Did Zoey put you up to this? I mean, having to do this at my age is embarrassing enough, and I don't know what she told you, but—"

He caught her hand. "I have no idea what you're talking about. Zoey hasn't said a thing to me." He barked a short laugh. "Believe me."

"Oh."

"Can I wait for you?"

"Well...I honestly will have only a few minutes. Maybe we should meet after my appointments. Who knows? I might even have something to celebrate."

That's what he was afraid of. "I'll tell you what. I'll walk you to wherever you're going and then wait for you."

"It may take an hour or longer."

"That's okay."

The look she gave him was wariness mixed with curiosity, but she nodded her agreement. "I'll be about twenty-five minutes in here. Shall we meet at the coffee bar?"

He smiled. "I'll have a cappuccino waiting for you."

"You could probably twist my arm," she said, smiling back.

Murmurings from inside the locker room grew louder, and they stepped away from the door to let a group of women out.

Haley led the pack, and as soon as she saw Adam her eyes lit up. "Hi," she said, and laid a familiar hand on his arm. "This is a surprise."

Without being rude, he casually shrugged away from her. He felt guilty when he shouldn't. "Hi, uh, Haley, isn't it?"

It was very quiet all of a sudden. One of the women she'd walked out with pressed her lips together and slid her other companion a quick look, and Adam figured he'd gotten the blonde's name wrong.

Haley blinked. "That's right." Lifting her chin, she

swept her hair off her shoulder. "I enjoyed lunch yesterday."

He'd started to turn to Gracie and briefly met her startled gaze. "Oh yeah. At the food court. Where we ran into each other. Unexpectedly." *Damn.* He sounded like a fifth-grade nerd.

"You know, I eat about the same time every day," Haley said, her voice subtly rising to an irritating pitch as she straightened and thrust her chest toward him.

Rubbing the side of his jaw, he shifted back a step. "Yeah, I guess that's good for your metabolism, or something." He turned to Gracie. "I'll see you in twenty-five, huh?"

She grinned, then without a word disappeared through the door of the locker room.

Not willing to be left alone with Haley and her smirking friends, Adam eyed the exit door. He uttered something totally inane, then missed Haley's reply as he beat it to the mall.

By the time he reached Cup-A-Chinos, he was laughing at himself. There was nothing to do but laugh. He'd gone from adolescent geek to scared rabbit back to adolescent in the span of five minutes.

And it was all because of Gracie.

He hadn't been himself since taking her home last week. Even the guys at work had commented on how distracted he was lately. His preoccupation was nothing he could explain. But he constantly found himself wondering about how her financial problem was being resolved or how her basement light was working.

His behavior was bizarre and irritating, and he had to do something about it.

It was clear he had to get her out of his system. That's why he'd decided to move in with her.

Chapter Eight

Gracie had just taken a sip of her cappuccino when Adam dropped the bomb. She gasped at the same time the foamy liquid gushed down her throat. She coughed, sputtered, recovered. Barely.

Adam frowned and took the glass mug from her shaky hands. "Are you okay?"

"No. Repeat what you just said."

"I think it makes sense for me to move in with you."

"To whom?"

"Think about it, Gracie. You need someone to share the house. I'm sick of living in a motel room. And I can fix things around the place." Uncertainty hovered at the edge of his smile, and she wondered who he was trying to convince. "Best of all, if we get on each other's nerves, it's not a long-term arrangement. I'll be leaving in about three months, anyway."

"Which will put me back to where I am now."

"Except that it'll buy you some time. You're in too big a rush right now. What if you end up with some crackpot?"

She arched a brow at him.

"With a friend like Zoey, you have the nerve to look at *me* like that?"

"Hey," she said, laughing. That was about the best defense she could muster. Zoey *was* a nut. Sobering, Gracie pursed her lips. "She did talk to you, didn't she?"

"Yeah, right. Zoey is going to bust a vein when she finds out we're living together."

"I didn't agree to anything." She almost said *yet*. But that was crazy. No way could they live together. Her pulse had gone berserk with the suggestion alone.

"Come on, Gracie. Admit it makes sense."

"It doesn't." She reached for her cappuccino, but her hands were still too unsteady and she folded them together.

His gaze snagged on the action before his eyes leveled on hers. "This would be purely platonic."

"I know that."

"Then what's the problem?"

"I'm looking for something…more permanent."

The guarded look that entered his eyes made her want to qualify what she'd said, to assure him that she wasn't talking about a relationship.

He nodded. "I understand," he said slowly, "but this arrangement will keep you from making a hasty decision."

"Why are you being so charitable?"

He smiled. "I'm not. My basic motive is purely selfish, believe me."

She leaned back in her chair as if she had all night. She didn't. She had to leave in three minutes.

He chuckled. "You want me to spell it out?"

"In detail."

He hesitated, the amusement slipping from his lips, and when his forehead creased in thought, she knew he was about to hedge. "It's simple. It's been a long time since I've lived anywhere but a motel room. I want a kitchen to cook in, and to be able to sit in a room I don't have to sleep in. And at the weekly rate the motel charges me, I'll probably be able to pay your entire mortgage and still come out ahead."

She shook her head. "We'll split it fairly," she said, and when his eyes glittered with hope, she realized how promising that sounded. Which was stupid, because it wasn't going to work. "But of course I haven't made up my mind. And to be honest, I doubt this is going to happen. I have an excellent candidate that I'm going to speak with—" she glanced at the wall clock "—in two minutes."

He stood when she did. "Promise me you won't finalize anything with this person without telling me."

"Adam, I don't—" She broke off when he captured her hand and stroked the inside of her wrist.

"Just give me five minutes rebuttal," he said, and when he smiled she felt her insides get all gooey like melted caramel.

"Okay," she said, even though nothing he could say would make her change her mind. Living with him for even an hour would be a disaster. Catastrophic. Foolish beyond words.

No way was Grace Louise Allen *that* stupid.

"WELL, MARY LOU, I think that about covers it, unless you have any more questions." Grace smiled at the polite, soft-spoken younger woman.

"There is one other thing." A shy pink crept into the woman's cheeks, and Gracie already liked her just because she was the only person Gracie knew who blushed more than she did. "I really like to cook and bake. And I have a real hankering for homemade ice cream, but I'm real good about cleaning up after myself. Would that be a problem?"

Homemade ice cream? Gracie massaged the ache blooming in her left temple. How could this woman be so perfect? She choked out a smile. "No problem at all."

Mary Lou smiled. Even her teeth were perfect. But then why shouldn't they be? The woman didn't smoke. Never had. Plus she detested loud music and spent her spare time reading. She was a member of a reader's group at the local library where she went three evenings a week, and on Sundays she taught a Bible class. She had no pets, although she was not averse to having one in the house. And, of course, she made homemade ice cream.

Gracie sighed. If she had one ounce of common sense left, she'd ask this woman to sign on the dotted line this very minute.

"Well, Mary Lou, how about if I get back to you tomorrow evening?" she asked, and when disappointment clouded the woman's eyes, she added, "I do have one more person I promised to talk with."

"I totally understand," Mary Lou said, and Gracie irritably thought that of course she did.

Both women stood, and Mary Lou extended her hand first. "I sure hope it works out. I like you, Gracie. You seem like a nice, honest, well-adjusted person.''

Color flooded Gracie's not so virtuous face as she accepted the woman's handshake. Wouldn't this Sunday school teacher be shocked to know where Gracie's thoughts had strayed through most of the interview? She didn't think the joy of living in sin was a topic Mary Lou ever covered with her Bible class.

Which, of course, was not what Adam was proposing. Gracie was the one who wanted to jump his bones. He wanted platonic.

Her face was still a little pink when she walked out of the oldies diner to meet Adam in the mall. She half expected him not to be there. She'd taken longer than she thought. Dwight hated to wait for anyone. If he had waited for her at all, it would have been to bite her head off.

She spotted Adam right away, though. He'd been sitting on a bench, jotting something in a small notebook, but as soon as he saw her he stuffed it into his jacket pocket and stood to meet her.

He hadn't been wearing the denim jacket before, it had been draped over his arm, but he had slipped into it while he'd waited, and she noticed how frayed it was at the cuffs and collar. It wasn't terribly noticeable, but it reminded her that he made his living doing odd jobs, which meant he didn't make a whole lot of money.

Maybe that's why he'd hedged earlier. He had mentioned that staying in a motel was costly, which she didn't doubt. And although he'd offered to pay her entire mortgage, that had probably been his pride speaking. Maybe he needed her to accept his offer more than she needed it. The thought gave her pause.

"I'm sorry I kept you waiting so long," she said as she approached him and noticed his slight frown.

"You're worth it." He winked, his lips curving in a roguish smile. "Besides, I had a lot to do."

"Such a charmer."

"Is it working?"

"I'll let you know after my ice cream."

"You're so easy," he said, slipping an arm around her shoulders as if it were the most natural thing in the world.

Leaning against him, she sighed before straightening and placing a respectable distance between them.

"How did the interview go?" he asked, only slightly loosening his hold.

"She's probably the best candidate yet."

He eyed her closely and frowned. "Looks like you made a decision."

She should have. The old Gracie would have snapped Mary Lou up and melted into a puddle of gratitude for having found someone who could be so compatible and bail her out of a financial problem at the same time. But the new one's pulse had leaped the moment she saw Adam's welcoming smile when he looked up and saw her coming.

He was right. She had made her decision, after all. Although it wasn't the enticement of jumping his bones or how nice she thought it would be to have him smile at her every day that swayed her. She thought about his frayed cuffs.

"I have," she said, feeling confident and more in

control than she had in ages. "Will you need help moving?"

GRACIE STIRRED the chicken gravy, spotted two lumps and fished them out just as the oven buzzer went off. The pies were done. After Adam got here and unpacked, all she had to do was make the mashed potatoes and heat everything that needed to be heated. The chicken and peas were also done, and she'd pulled leftover biscuits out of the freezer.

"Well, aren't we little Miss Suzy Homemaker?" Zoey strolled in and plucked off a piece of crisp golden chicken.

Gracie slapped her hand. "Did you have to take it off the top?"

Zoey glared at her. "I can't believe you're going to all this trouble. And I sure as hell can't believe you're letting him move in."

"It's strictly business."

Zoey eyed the apple pies. "Right."

"That's not fair. Don't I make apple pies three times a year and always in October?"

"Yeah, but you usually invite us over."

Gracie laughed. "So that's your problem."

"My problem is that you're letting some stranger, who could be a serial killer, for all we know, move in and have free rein. Your parents would have a fit if they knew."

"My parents aren't going to know." Gracie wiped her hands on her apron and gave her friend a meaningful look. "Are they?"

"I won't lie to them if they ask."

"Zoey." Gracie drawled her warning. "If you're not going to behave while Adam is here, then leave."

"I can't believe this. Even though I knew it would happen, I can't believe it. You're actually putting a man before our friendship."

Gracie's hands froze in the middle of untying her apron, and she stared at her friend. "You don't really believe that, do you?"

Zoey shrugged sheepishly and broke off a piece of pie crust.

"I love you like a sister, Zoey. You know me better than one. I have never nor would I ever let anyone interfere with our friendship. But you have been impossible lately. And I'm just trying to keep the peace."

"I know." Zoey nibbled the chunk of crust. "I'm sorry I said that."

Gracie sighed and yanked off her apron. "I thought you'd be proud of me. I'm not moping over Dwight. Instead, I'm getting on with my life. And I've told you at least ten times, there is nothing physical between Adam and I. We're friends."

"Then why are you turning so red?"

"If you really want to know, it's because I'd get him in the sack in a heartbeat, but he's not interested."

Zoey's jaw just about hit the floor the same time the doorbell rang. Gracie's hand automatically flew up to smooth her hair. Her friend's mouth opened and closed, then opened again. Nothing but a sputter emerged. It sounded a lot like a sick cat.

"We'll discuss this later," Gracie whispered, flashing her a warning look, then headed for the front door.

Her smile promptly vanished when she saw who was standing there.

"I didn't think I should use my key," Dwight said.

"You're right." Gracie took a deep breath and stepped aside for him to enter. Once he passed her, she stuck her head out the door and peered down the street. The leaves of the tree-lined road were starting to change to brilliant oranges and pinks. But no sign of Adam's truck.

"Expecting someone?" Dwight asked when she closed the door against the fall chill and turned to face him.

"Yes, I am."

"Hi, Dwight." Zoey sauntered into the room, her gaze darting nervously from him to Gracie, and Gracie no longer had to ask her next question.

She smiled at them both before focusing on him. "Well, now that I know why you're here, when are you leaving?"

Her ex-fiancé's eyes narrowed. "What's happened to you?"

"You mean, I used to be such a nice girl?"

"Something like that."

"I think the correct term is pushover. It got tiring." Gracie smiled and tamped down her resentments. Replaying old tapes wouldn't do any good. She knew that. But it was hard to stand here looking at Dwight and not recall all the times he'd ignored her, the times he'd laughed on the phone with his friends while she sat alone in the living room.

His blond hair was slightly disheveled, the way it usually was. She used to find that endearing. Now she wanted to hand him a comb.

"Did you want anything specific?" she asked when the silence had grown too long.

"I think maybe I left some computer games in the basement," he said, and she smiled because she remembered another reason she was glad he didn't live here anymore.

"I don't recall seeing any, but go have a look."

He sniffed the air. "That time of year again, huh?" His eyes briefly closed, and when he opened them, there was a spark of fondness there that made her remember better times. "You always made the best pies, Gracie."

She started to return to the kitchen and made it as far as the dining room. She stopped at the arched doorway to look at him. "Thank you," she said, and out of the corner of her eye, she caught Zoey beaming at them. And why shouldn't she? This was the Dwight her friend knew. The one she thought Gracie was a fool to give up on. "Dwight?"

"Yeah, Gracie?" He stepped forward.

"Don't forget to leave your key."

She walked calmly through the dining room, careful not to look at her friend, and as soon as she made it to the kitchen, she sagged against the counter.

Why couldn't Zoey let this go? Maybe Gracie had been wrong to be so circumspect about the deterioration of their relationship. Of course, she had shared many of her complaints with Zoey, but she hadn't wanted to dump on Dwight too much, either. That wouldn't have been fair, because he was Zoey and Brian's friend, too.

She had to have a heart to heart with Zoey. There was no getting around it. Adam was going to be here at any minute, and he was going to live here for the next three months or however long he decided to stay. And Gracie couldn't stand it if there was tension between him and her best friend.

While listening with half an ear on what was happening in the other room, she loaded everything she could into the oven and started cleaning the counters. As soon as the front door slammed, Zoey appeared in the kitchen.

Gracie held up a hand. "Before you say one word—"

"You're right. I'm proud of you."

"What?"

Zoey squinted. "What happened to the pies?" She picked up a bunched-up dish towel, and finding nothing under it, frowned, "What did you do with them?"

Chuckling, Gracie reached into the built-in bread pantry and pulled out a foil-wrapped pan. She placed it on the counter. "This one goes home with you. Demolish that crust if you want."

She grinned. "I knew you wouldn't fail me."

"Of course not."

Zoey's sheepish sidelong gaze swept Gracie. "About our conversation earlier—"

"Forget it."

"I was being a selfish twit, I admit. And I think Dwight has probably needed a kick in the butt for a long time. But I don't want to see you get hurt again, either."

"Adam's moving in isn't the same thing."

"It *shouldn't* be."

"And it isn't."

"You said yourself you wanted to get him in the sack."

Gracie scowled at her friend. "And why did you ask Todd at the sporting goods store if he'd turned eighteen yet? Correct me if I'm wrong, but I don't think your interest had anything to do with getting him a birthday present. Is that any different?"

"Damn right, it's different. That would be pure sex."

Gracie stuck the biscuits in the toaster oven and whirled toward her friend. "Well, what do you think—"

Her words shriveled and died in her mouth and made a painful journey down the back of her throat.

Over Zoey's left shoulder, standing just outside the kitchen, Adam put up a hand in greeting.

Zoey spun to see what had Gracie so tongue-tied and let out a shriek.

Adam's expression shifted from unreadable to startled. "I knocked," he said, "twice. The door was open." He shrugged, and when no one said anything, he pointed toward the front door and asked, "Shall I come back later?"

Gracie quickly wiped her hands on the dish towel. *Oh, God, this couldn't really be happening.* "No, of course not. You just surprised us, that's all." She slid Zoey a warning look as she headed out of the kitchen. "I'll help you bring your things in."

He backed up to make room for her. "No need. Both my bags are on the porch. If you'd just point me to the right room…"

"Yeah, I'd like to see that, too," Zoey said as she waltzed past them, her nose reaching for the ceiling.

"You're forgetting your pie," Gracie reminded her in a dry tone.

"I'm not leaving yet."

Gracie snagged her arm and yanked her back. "Yes, you are," she said sweetly. She grabbed the foil-wrapped pan off the counter and pushed it into her friend's hands. "See you tomorrow, Zoey."

Adam left the doorway, but not before Gracie caught the grin tugging at his lips.

Zoey opened her mouth to protest, but Gracie ushered her to the back door. "Goodbye, Zoey."

"I can't believe you're kicking me out of your house."

"One more word, and I take back the pie."

Cradling her bounty with one hand while grumbling under her breath, Zoey reached into her jeans pocket and pulled out her keys. "Call me."

"I will."

"Tonight."

Gracie closed the door and shook her head. Maybe she should have invited Zoey and Brian over for dinner. Maybe if they got to know Adam a little Zoey wouldn't worry so much. But that wouldn't have been right, either. It would have seemed like a double date, when actually Adam was simply a tenant moving in.

When she got to the living room, Adam was standing at the foot of the stairs, a suitcase in one hand, a duffel bag in the other.

"I'm sorry if I came at a bad—"

"I'm sorry about Zoey—"

They both spoke at once and stopped.

Adam grinned. "I won't be sorry if you won't."

Gracie laughed. "Zoey is going to be the sorry one

if she doesn't knock it off,'' she said, and headed up the stairs.

"She's your friend. It's her job to be protective.''

Adam's voice came from directly behind her, and she was suddenly aware of how close he was, following her up the narrow stairs…undoubtedly staring at her fat behind. She straightened her spine and tried to inconspicuously tuck her fanny muscles.

"She'll get over it.'' She arrived at the top and stepped aside to wait for him. "She just doesn't understand our relationship. Somehow she sees you as replacing Dwight, and it's hard for her to get past that. But she will.''

As he got to the top step, she veered to the right and pushed open his bedroom door. "This is it,'' she said. "If you don't like the colors or the comforter, feel free to change them.''

Instead of continuing into the room, Adam stood beside her and set down his bags. He stared at the queen-size bed for several long seconds, offering no comment, his face arranged in a thoughtful frown, making her wonder if the tans and blues and the walnut furniture made the room look too dark and unappealing.

Finally, he looked away from the bed and straight into her eyes. "Is this a good idea?'' he asked.

"We can change the paint if you want.''

"That's not what I mean.''

"I'll talk to Zoey.''

A tolerant, almost condescending smile played about his mouth, and her heart sunk. He'd obviously overheard her conversation with Zoey. Heat burned its way up her neck and into her cheeks.

He raised his hands to cup her shoulders. He didn't have to reach far. He was close, almost kissing close, and she would have backed up, but there was no place for her to go. "I wouldn't care if the room was pea green, and Zoey I can handle, but you've been jumpy ever since I got here. Are you having second thoughts?"

"I'm not jumpy."

He touched the tip of her nose. "You're also beet red."

"Thank you for pointing that out."

He grinned. "Wow, it's only the first day, and I'm already getting dished up the sarcasm."

Her cheeks grew warmer. "Sorry. Maybe I am jumpy, but it has nothing to do with you."

Nudging her chin with his forefinger, he ducked his head to stare into her eyes. "Honest?"

"Honest."

His gaze dropped to her mouth. "You're jumpy right now."

She stared back, helpless to think up a reply, helpless to think about anything other than the fullness of his lower lip, the way his right cheek grooved when amusement tugged at his mouth. The way her heart was beating so fast it made her dizzy.

"The pies," she said finally.

His gaze stayed fastened on her face. "What pies?"

"They're in the oven and I don't remember if I set the timer and that's why I'm jumpy."

Slowly, hypnotically, the groove deepened in his cheek as a leisurely smile curved his lips. "You want me to go check them?"

The trance was broken. She jerked back. "No. I'll do that. You settle in."

"Gracie?"

She swallowed. "Yes."

"We're friends, right?" He moved slightly closer.

He was going to hug her again. Her pulse scrambled to regain its rhythm. She nodded briskly and sucked in her stomach.

"So any time there's anything wrong...and it involves me, you'll tell me?" He leaned down to pick up his duffel bag without touching her.

She moved out of the way and released her stomach muscles. "Of course. I better go check the pies."

"It'll only take me a couple of minutes to unpack."

"I have soda and beer in the fridge," she said, backing down the hall.

"I'll be there in a minute."

Gracie had already started racing down the stairs. When she got to the kitchen, she jerked everything out of the oven while she called herself every sophomoric name she could come up with.

She hadn't acted this idiotic in high school. Maybe Zoey was right. Maybe Gracie wasn't thinking too clearly. On the other hand, she thought, as she set her best stoneware on the dining room table, if she just laid her cards on the table with Adam, maybe they could have a few quick rolls in the hay, she could get it out of her system, and they could go on with the business of being housemates.

Rolls in the hay. What was she thinking? She glanced despairingly at the ceiling. And noticed that one of the dining room chandelier bulbs was burned out. She rushed to the buffet, and from the drawer she withdrew two tapered vanilla candles.

She was fairly sure that he was reasonably attracted to her. He at least liked her. They were both adults....

She arranged the candles in the center of the table, returned to the kitchen, flipped on the toaster oven to heat the biscuits, then fished the boiled potatoes out of the pot. The gravy continued to simmer, and as soon as she was done whipping the potatoes, dinner would be ready.

She could give him subtle hints and see how he responded. That was hardly laying her cards on the table, she knew, but then again, if she'd read the situation wrong, she wouldn't look like a total buffoon.

The electric hand mixer was going full blast when she felt the gentle pressure at her waist. Starting, she flipped off the switch and looked into Adam's dark chocolate eyes.

He let his hand drop and stepped back. "Sorry, I seem to keep startling you. But you didn't hear me calling."

She looked at his boots and wondered why he was still wearing them.

Catching her interest, he said, "I promise the bottoms are clean."

"Oh, no, I wasn't worried about that." She set down the mixer and smiled. He looked as though he might have just shaved.

"I found a key on the nightstand. I take it it belongs to the front door."

"Front and back."

He nodded, his gaze straying toward the dining room table. Plates were stacked, linen napkins and silverware lying beside them, the candles not yet lighted.

"I see you're having company," he said, and she blinked. "I won't be in your way. I have to go back to work."

"Oh."

"I'll probably be back late." He moved to the doorway. "But I'll be quiet."

"You won't disturb me." She shoved the potatoes aside.

"Okay." His gaze again drifted toward the table before he disappeared.

Gracie put the potatoes in the sink and stared out the back window for a good ten minutes. Then she fixed a small plate and lit the candles while the food heated in the microwave. And then she sat at the table and did what she always did. She ate alone.

Chapter Nine

Adam was dead tired by the time he pulled up to Gracie's house. The outside lamp was on, flooding the porch with a light so soft and yellow that it was hard to see the chipped white paint flaking off the stair railing. A lamp burned in the living room, too, but the rest of the house was as black as freshly mined coal.

For a moment he thought he saw a light flicker from the second floor, but he blinked and it was gone, probably an invention of his imagination. He'd harbored a small fantasy for most of the night that Gracie would wait up for him. But he hadn't really expected her to. He figured that she might have had a date.

It was Saturday night, after all, and she'd gone through a lot of trouble to make dinner for someone.

He hoped that someone wasn't Dwight.

And then he reminded himself that it was none of his business.

So why had he spent most of the night going nuts, wondering what she was up to? After convincing half the construction crew to pull a night shift, he'd felt obligated to stick around in case they had any questions. But his mind hadn't been on business. It had been on Gracie. And who was making her blush.

That's when he'd jumped into the fray, hauling bricks, getting as physical as he possibly could. That the men had been surprised he'd actually gotten his hands dirty told him how far he'd shifted away from the business he used to love. They had all teased him, pretending they were concerned for his advanced age, and the more they taunted the harder he'd pushed. All he had to show for it were aching muscles and dirty fingernails. Well, he'd quickly gotten rid of the dirt. The wicked backache he was going to have to live with for a while.

He grabbed a paper bag from the passenger side and wearily clambered out of his truck. As he climbed the porch steps, he made a mental note to sand down the railing so he could slap on some fresh paint. The mall job was eating up all his time now, but later, when it was complete...

He shoved a hand roughly through his hair before fumbling with the key. Later, he'd have another job in another city, and he couldn't be worried about Gracie's porch. Or Gracie.

After two tries he managed to open the door without spilling his bag. He tried to be as quiet as possible. Although it was only ten-fifteen, if she wasn't out, she was obviously asleep.

He started to head for the kitchen but stopped and stared balefully at his boots. Clean they may have been when he'd left, but no telling what they'd picked up tonight. He set down the bag and grimaced as he stooped to untie his laces. His back muscles screamed with protest. He wasn't that out of shape. In fact, he wasn't out of shape at all. He couldn't figure out what he'd done to himself to be in this much agony. He hoped Gracie had a firm mattress.

Thinking about Gracie and mattresses put a whole new twist on his problem, and the curse he bit out was succinct but heartfelt. That had been his trouble. He'd done too much lifting without paying attention to what he was doing. He'd been thinking about Gracie and sheet-tangling and…and damn it, he knew better than that.

He kicked off his boots, straightened with a groan, then continued to the kitchen with his bag.

By the time he'd deposited the contents, the freezer door could barely close. He grabbed a beer out of the fridge and saw the plastic-wrapped plates of food crammed into every available spot. Whoever had come over for dinner sure hadn't eaten much.

He, on the other hand, was starving and wondered how far his new landlord's goodwill extended.

"There's plenty of leftovers if you're hungry," she said from behind him.

Startled, he straightened suddenly, and a sharp pain sliced across his lower back.

"Son of a—" He cut his words off and turned in time to see her worry her lower lip.

Her hair was tousled as if she'd just gotten out of bed, her eyes a little hazy with sleep, and below the hem of her fuzzy pink robe, her feet were bare.

"What's wrong?" she asked.

"Nothing." He tried to smile. It came out a scowl. "I guess my back's a little sore."

"From what?"

"From working."

"You were at work?"

"Yeah." He frowned. "Didn't I tell you I had to work?"

Clearing her throat, she swept past him. "You might have mentioned it. Did you eat?"

"I didn't have time."

A frown puckered her brows as she reached into a cabinet and brought down a plate. "They work you too hard. We have chicken, biscuits, peas." She paused, the frown deepening. "No mashed potatoes, but pie for dessert."

Adam leaned against the counter and watched her thoughtfully while he sipped his beer. He knew now why he'd hightailed it out of here after unpacking. It wasn't because he wanted to stay out of her way if she had company. Hell, she might have even cooked the dinner for him. And he hadn't returned to work strictly out of dedication to his job.

He'd gotten cold feet. Gracie was a nice lady. She looked content bustling around her kitchen, and she looked good in her plain pink robe. She needed a nice husband. She needed kids who behaved and did their homework. What she didn't need was a vagabond like him who could offer her nothing but a couple of months of friendship, maybe some hot sex and home repairs. Gracie needed someone to share her home. And her bed.

"You aren't cooperating," she said, holding a plate of chicken in one hand, biscuits in the other, and he realized he hadn't heard a word she'd said.

"Hey, don't wait on me, Gracie." He pushed off the counter to take the food from her, and another cramp clenched a back muscle.

Her eyes widened at his expression, and she slid both plates onto the counter. "Your back is more than a little sore, isn't it?"

"It'll go away."

"No doubt, but that doesn't mean we can't do something for it in the meantime." She glanced at the microwave's digital clock and made a face. "I'm not sure I have anything, and the drugstores just closed."

"I know." He took a pull of beer.

She squinted at the hand he had wrapped around the bottle. "What's wrong with your thumb?"

He transferred the beer to his other hand and held up his splayed fingers for inspection. The thumb had started to swell. "I sort of banged it."

"Rough night, huh?" Casting him a curious sidelong glance, she yanked open the freezer door. "Some ice will help that." She started to reach for the ice bin and stopped to dart him a look of disbelief. "Where did all this come from?"

Several quarts of ice cream were stacked haphazardly atop each other, occupying every available space and obscuring the ice bin. She pulled out a carton of strawberry and quickly caught a quart of butter pecan when it started to topple.

"Did you just put these in here?" she asked when he didn't reply.

"Well, yeah." He shrugged at her frown. It had seemed like a good idea a half hour ago.

Her troubled gaze went to the carton labels as she stacked one quart after another on the counter. Adam had picked up hand-dipped goodies from a popular ice cream parlor near town. Apparently, she wasn't fond of that particular store because she looked kind of funny. Maybe even a little upset.

"If you don't like those flavors, there are more in the back," he said, watching her warily. He'd done something wrong. That was clear. But for the life of him, he couldn't figure out what that was. "And if you don't like any of them, well, no problem."

She pressed her lips together, finally reached the ice bin and withdrew it from the freezer. When she turned to him, she looked suspiciously misty eyed. "I like them all. Thank you." She smiled. "Let's get some ice on that thumb. Then I'll go dig out a heating pad for your back."

He groaned. "An ice pack, a heating pad…you make me sound like an old geezer."

She lifted a brow. "No, an old geezer would have more sense than to get banged up like this. What did they make you do tonight, anyway?"

Her question stopped him. It had been a long time since anyone had made him do anything. But then he remembered that she didn't know he was the boss. She thought he was some kind of laborer. He smiled. He wasn't sure why her misconception pleased him so much or why he hadn't corrected her false assumption. Even his mother hadn't gotten over the fact that he wasn't a Harvard graduate. He had a feeling Gracie wouldn't care if he'd been a high-school dropout.

"We're behind schedule," he said simply. "Everyone is really hauling butt to get the job done."

"Killing you guys isn't going to accomplish that. Here," she said, pressing the small plastic bag of ice she'd prepared against his thumb. "Use this dish towel and keep it wrapped while I go hunt down the heating pad. This plate of chicken and biscuits is ready to be heated in the microwave, too.''

''Gracie?''

She'd made it as far as the door and stopped to look at him. Her eyes weren't hazy anymore, they were bright and focused and full of determination. And her smile. God, he loved her smile. It was enough to make his back feel better already.

''Were you ever in the military?'' he asked.

Her smile faltered, and her brows drew sharply together.

The grin he'd been trying to hold in check stretched across his face, and she promptly clued in to his teasing.

''Listen, buster, come tomorrow morning, you'll be darn glad I'm making you take care of yourself,'' she said, waving him off as she retreated.

''You need some kids, Gracie,'' he called out, laughing. ''A whole bunch to boss around.''

Gracie kept walking, but she slowed down, tempted to ask him if he were volunteering. She chuckled to herself, thinking about the look on his face if she did. But she hadn't gone quite that far off the deep end. She picked up her pace.

She couldn't lose the silly grin, though. The one that kept popping in place every time she thought about what he'd done. He'd brought her ice cream. And although that gesture was sweet all by itself, he'd deliberately chosen the ice cream over the drugstore. Gracie knew they both closed at ten.

It was a stupid, impractical decision to make. And she ought to give him a good scolding.

She started grinning all over again as she located the heating pad, then rummaged through her medicine cabinet in case there was some muscle cream she'd forgotten she had. No luck.

When she returned downstairs, Adam was standing at the counter, wolfing down a chicken leg.

"Does it hurt too much to sit?" she asked, worried again.

Wiping a napkin across his mouth, he looked up. "No. I was too hungry to get to the table." His gaze dropped to the heating pad. "Great. You found it."

"After you're done eating, shall we hook you up in the living room?

"Hook me up?" He pushed the chicken aside and shot her a hesitant glance. "That sounds so...so ominous."

She laughed. "It's only a figure of speech."

"You just plug it in and lay it on my back, right?" He didn't look convinced. "I've never used one before."

"That's it. Simple."

"Do I need to take off my shirt?"

Gracie opened her mouth to correct him, then promptly closed it. She stared into his expectant eyes for several long seconds, mentally debating her new opportunity. She really shouldn't take advantage of the situation, but on the other hand, what he didn't know... "Yes, that would be very helpful."

He nodded and plucked at a shirt button.

"But you can finish eating first," she said, and immediately swiveled to fuss with the food on the counter so he wouldn't see the blush sweeping her face.

"Nah, I think I'd better get this over with. Did we decide on the living room?"

"Sure." She pushed back her hair, took a deep breath and turned.

He had only one button left to go. Beneath his red flannel shirt, he wore a white T-shirt. She stared at the second barrier and tried not to laugh. She was so pitifully bad at this seduction stuff. Someone needed to come out with a flirting book. They'd make a fortune.

Adam pulled off the flannel shirt, looked around for a moment, then threw it over the back of a dining room chair. He caught her eyeing him and said, "I'll pick this up before I go upstairs."

"Don't worry about it." She blinked, and her gaze dropped to his white shirt. He reached for the hem and drew it over his head.

His broad chest was remarkably tanned for October, and his pecs were firm and well-developed. Subtle ridges of muscle defined his flat stomach, and a smattering of silky black hair fanned out just above his belt buckle.

And Gracie was darn glad she had the counter to lean on.

"The couch okay?" he asked.

"Fine."

It wasn't her voice that squeaked past her lips, but if Adam noticed, he didn't comment. He took another quick sip of beer, left the bottle in the sink and headed for the living room with his ice pack still pressed to his thumb.

She should be ashamed of herself, Gracie briefly considered. The poor guy was wounded, and here she was looking at him as if he were dessert. She paused only a second before grabbing two more beers out of the fridge, then followed him.

"You didn't know a tenant could be so much trouble, did you?" he asked with a rueful grin, and sat down.

"Here." She handed him both beers. "Open these while I find an outlet."

"What is this? Anesthetic?"

"Don't be a baby. One of those is for me."

He twisted off the caps, then narrowed his gaze between her and the heating pad. "Is this going to be one of those 'it's going to hurt me more than it will you' deals?"

"It can be, if you don't grow up."

"Ouch. Remind me never to wake you up before noon."

She bent over to plug in the heating pad, and as she straightened, she caught him staring at her fanny.

He looked up suddenly, his guilty eyes briefly meeting hers. "I can figure this out. Why don't you go back to bed?"

"I hadn't fallen asleep yet. I was reading. Now, turn over."

He placed both beers on the side table. "Yes, ma'am."

She was proud of herself. She'd gotten quite an eyeful of him so far, and she hadn't drooled once, but as soon as he flipped onto his stomach, she reached for a sip of beer.

My, oh, my. He had a fine butt. The denim of his jeans was worn in just the right places, the soft material cupping him to perfection. He looked firm and taut and had just the right amount of curve and dip, and her fluffy robe suddenly felt stiflingly hot.

Her robe? The pink one? She looked at herself and nearly groaned. How could she have been so asinine as to have grabbed the first thing off the hook? She looked like her mother.

He frowned over his shoulder at her. "Am I supposed to be doing something else?"

She snapped to attention. "Where does it hurt? Your lower back?"

"Right here." He twisted to show her and grimaced with pain.

She could see where the muscles had tightened and knotted, and she gently probed the area with the tips of her fingers. He flinched at the contact.

She yanked back her hand. "I'm sorry. Did that hurt?"

He shook his head, keeping his gaze forward. "I didn't expect it. Go ahead."

"I'm going to lay the heating pad on your back now. It'll be warm enough in no time." Touching first one finger, then another to the pad, she pursed her lips, then pressed her entire palm flush against the felt-like material. It wasn't nearly as warm as it should be.

"No, I meant go ahead with the massage."

She looked at him, confused. He didn't turn around. His chin rested on his folded hands. "I wasn't going to give you a massage."

"Whatever you did felt awfully good."

"Right. That's why you jumped."

"From sheer pleasure, Gracie, sheer pleasure."

She heard the grin in his voice, and she smiled,

too. Feeling more confident, she unplugged the pad and set it aside then flexed her fingers. It was a lot easier to be bold when she didn't have to look him in the eyes. Truth be told, she had been trained as a masseuse the same time she'd taken up aerobics. It had been almost ten years since she'd passed her state board exams, and she was more than a little rusty....

She quit flexing and balled her fists around the collar of her robe, squeezing the lapels together. What was she, crazy? She couldn't do this. This was like having only one lick of an ice cream cone, like peeling one tiny slab of chocolate off a candy bar. This was totally nuts.

So when did one little lick hurt anyone? Even if she were on a diet, she'd have one small, itsy-bitsy lick.

Besides, maybe all he needed was to work out some of the kinks. How could she refuse him this small relief? She stared at the broad expanse of tanned skin and swallowed.

The coffee table made the area too cramped for her to work, so she pushed it back, sunk to her knees and wiggled into a comfortable position.

"Maybe we ought to do this upstairs where there's more room?" Adam craned his neck to look at her, and she thumped him gently on his head.

"Quit twisting around. You'll make matters worse." *Not to mention disconcert the heck out of me.*

"I don't want you to have to kneel on the hard floor. The bed would be much better."

"Much," she repeated, not bothering to hide her sarcasm. "Now, keep still."

"Yes, ma'am."

Hearing the laughter in his voice, she relaxed a little. He was so easy to be around that sometimes she forgot she really didn't know him at all. But as he'd often pointed out, they were just friends.

Again, she flexed her hands. And again she told herself that she could do this.

"Tell me as soon as anything hurts," she ordered as she gently laid her hands on him.

"Ah." He made the word three syllables, and she snatched back her hands. "Don't stop."

"I did hurt you."

"Ah, Gracie." Adam reached an arm behind him and blindly groped. Catching one of her hands, he placed it near his waist. "Trust me. You didn't injure me in any way, shape or form."

His voice sounded a little funny, and she wasn't sure she should trust him at all. Maybe he just didn't want to hurt her feelings.

"But…"

"Gracie."

She let the palm of the hand he'd placed on his back sink against him. After testing a small amount of pressure, she added her other hand, the heel of her palm coming to rest firmly on the small of his back.

His skin was warm and smooth, and she wondered if her hands were too cold. She let up on some of the pressure. "Adam? If my hands are too—"

"Gracie, if your hands don't stay on my back, you're in trouble. Period. Did that answer your question?"

"Uh, I think so." His gruff tone took her by surprise, and she frowned at the back of his head.

His shoulders moved with the big breath he took. "I didn't mean to sound snappy."

"Maybe this wasn't such a good idea."

He flipped over almost before the last word was out of her mouth, and she found both her palms flat against his chest. Smack dab in the center of her left hand, his nipple beaded against her palm. She blinked and started to pull away.

He caught both her wrists, and from the way his expression briefly twisted, she knew he'd strained his back. She froze, not wanting to cause him additional injury.

"I'm sorry," she said, her voice coming out ragged and breathless. "You startled me."

"Then I guess I should apologize." His gaze roamed her face. "But I don't feel particularly apologetic right now."

Her wrists remained imprisoned, and she relaxed her hands against his chest. The rest of her body was another matter. Her entire nervous system was as taut as a violin string ready to pop. Her pulse was zigging when she was certain it should be zagging, and her mouth was as dry as the Sahara.

Extremely glad she was already on her knees, she leaned against the couch, hoping her sudden light-headedness would subside. The action brought her face closer to his, and he smiled.

"I'm supposed to be giving you a massage," she said, her gaze hopelessly tangled with his.

He let go one of her wrists to brush a strand of hair from her cheek. His touch made her tingle, and while she should have seized the opportunity to remove her hand from his chest, she stayed where she was.

"Don't let me stop you."

His gaze held hers for a long moment, then she dropped hers to his chest. "You're facing the wrong way."

"I know. The problem is, you keep pulling away."

"What if I promise not to do that any more?" she asked, refusing to look at him.

With his knuckles, he nudged her chin up until she was forced to meet his eyes. "You're doing it already."

"I'm not sure about what's happening here," she said honestly.

"I'm not, either." His hand slid from her jaw to the back of her neck.

Her hair fell forward, shuttering her face, and she closed her eyes to drink in the exquisite feel of his palm cupping her neck and compelling her toward him.

"Gracie?"

His hand was so warm and strong, and his mouth was close enough that she could feel his breath dance across her cheek. She wanted him to kiss her. She didn't want him to break the spell by asking. If she didn't answer, maybe he would just...

"Gracie?"

"Hmm?"

"Open your eyes."

Something in his tone sparked a flicker of panic in her heart, and she quickly did as he asked.

His eyes were darker than midnight, steady and focused on her face, and before she could blink, disappointment flashed through them as quick as lightning.

Then a sad smile lifted the corners of his mouth, and leaning forward, he brushed his lips across her forehead.

Chapter Ten

She wasn't ready, Adam realized. He was. He was so ready he thought he might pop something at any minute. But when Gracie opened her eyes and he witnessed her panic at realizing who she was with, his suspicion was confirmed.

She obviously still had feelings for Dwight.

And Adam wasn't in the mood to play substitute lover.

He knew he'd been foolish to think the massage was any type of a come-on. She treated him like a brother most of the time. Yet occasionally a mixed signal seeped through the cracks, and although he normally was able to ignore them, like a damn fool, this time he'd acted on impulse. And something a little more basic.

Sighing, he released her neck and patted her shoulder. He really was extremely sore, and it wasn't as if he would have been able to do much, anyway. She might even have kicked him out for poor performance. Not that her thoughts—or hormones—were even remotely aligned with his.

His hand slipped from her, and he leaned against

the couch. From the vee of her robe to the parting of her hair, she was flushed with color, making her eyes look incredibly blue and heart-stoppingly beautiful. He wasn't surprised that she was reacting this way. She often blushed when she was nervous or embarrassed. He did feel bad, however, for causing her discomfort.

He put a hand over hers, pausing, searching for the right words. "Gracie?"

Her eyes promptly narrowed, and she jerked from his touch. He realized she wasn't embarrassed. She was ticked.

"Don't Gracie me," she said, her eyes bright with temper. "Come here." Grabbing him awkwardly by the shoulders, she hauled him to her and kissed him hard on the mouth.

When she released him, he slumped against the couch, stunned, speechless, trying to grasp what had just happened. He knew one thing for sure. That was no sisterly kiss.

She sat back, bumping against the coffee table, looking as surprised as he was.

"I don't know what I did to deserve that, but I must be living right." He half-laughed, half-grinned.

She stared, looking shell-shocked, for almost a minute. "Shut up, Adam." She tried to scramble to her feet but got trapped between the couch and the coffee table.

Taking full advantage of her predicament, he captured her forearm. Somehow, his hand burrowed beneath the wide sleeve of her robe. Her skin felt smooth and silky under his grip.

"I'm sorry I did that," she said. "Now will you kindly let go of me."

"Not until we discuss what just happened."

"You're kidding."

"Nope."

"Oh, swell," she said, throwing up her free hand and trying unsuccessfully to stand. "Every woman on this planet knows that getting a man to talk is like trying to make brownies without fat grams, and I get one that wants to discuss a stupid k—"

The word clearly stuck in her mouth, and she sank down with a mutinous look on her face he'd never seen before. She said, "There's nothing to discuss."

"This is a fascinating new side I'm seeing." Keeping a firm grip on her, he struggled to a sitting position. The effort cost him, but he tried to keep the pain from reaching his expression.

Her face softened. "Let me help you."

"I'm okay, but it would make it easier if you would sit here next to me."

She nodded, and he let her arm go so he could lean back in a more comfortable position. Clutching the corner of the coffee table, she hoisted herself up. Her robe parted, displaying a long, bare leg, and Adam did all he could to keep from angling for a better look.

His heart jerked off rhythm, and his entire body recalled their brief but hard kiss. By the time she'd straightened her robe and settled beside him, he felt himself growing hard all over again.

Folding his hands across his lap, he said, "If I asked for that, how can I do it again?"

"Not funny." She let her head fall back and stared

miserably at the ceiling. "This is your first night here, and I blow it."

He started to make a crack, then decided she wouldn't appreciate the first thought that had come to mind. "I'm the one who almost blew it. You had the good sense not to let an opportunity pass."

She half-grunted, half-sighed, as if she didn't believe him. Then she brought her head up and met his gaze. "So, why did you?"

He hesitated, wondering how frank he should be. Then he remembered he was talking to Gracie. She deserved honesty.

"Dwight."

A frown replaced her initial surprise. "What does he have to do with anything?"

"You can't live with a guy for as long as you did and still not have feelings for him."

"Why not?" She averted her face to stare at her hands. "I lived with my brother for longer than I lived with Dwight."

"That's not the same thing."

"Yes, it is."

"Gracie, you know what I'm saying."

"Yes." She plucked at a loose thread on her robe.

"You mean you and Dwight didn't—"

She shook her head without looking at him. "For the last year and a half, anyway."

He felt relieved and outraged at the same time. And then he felt guilty for being so damn happy. He wondered if Zoey knew about this. "I'm sorry for prying. That wasn't my intention."

She shrugged. "I volunteered."

He watched as she seemed to clam up. She looked

different all of a sudden, certainly not like the same confident, spunky woman who had grabbed him and kissed him only minutes ago.

"You don't think that was your fault, do you?" he asked warily.

Her chin lifted. "Not totally."

"I mean, you may not have wanted that kind of relationship, but speaking strictly from a male point of view, you—"

Her reaction was physical and abrupt. She stood, nearly knocking the coffee table over. "This is a very odd conversation, and I think you'll understand why I don't want to have it."

He pushed to his feet, too, but with far greater effort. "Let's not go to bed angry, Gracie."

She'd already made it around the couch, but she stopped, her eyes widening. "I'm not mad." Her smile was wan. "It's old news, and it's not worth dragging up again."

"It is if it makes you feel bad."

She held up a single finger, pleading for silence.

"Okay." He smiled, making his way around the couch to stand in front of her. "I'll shut up. But where does this leave us?"

The question was rhetorical. He knew nothing was going to happen now. While he was glad he didn't have to compete with Dwight or his ghost, he had another problem. If he tried anything romantic, she'd think he was trying to prove something.

A tiny frown puckered her brows, and he could tell she was trying to decide if she could get away with deliberately misunderstanding. That would be hard to do after that kiss she'd laid on him. Whether she wanted to admit it or not, that kiss had changed things between them.

Finally her features relaxed a little. "Still friends?"

Yeah, right. But this wasn't the time to push her. "Still friends," he agreed, and shifted uncomfortably against his straining fly.

She started to head for the stairs and glanced over her shoulder. "What about your back?"

"It feels much better. Go on to bed, Gracie."

She gave him a sweet little smile and turned away.

As he watched her go he figured it was a good thing he wasn't looking for a relationship. Because if he was, he'd sure have his hands full with Gracie.

"HOW'S THE HOUSE playing going?" Zoey asked before she dived into her banana nut muffin.

That was the third irritating time in the week since Adam had moved in that her friend had asked her that question, and Gracie felt no obligation to reply.

Besides, Adam living under the same roof with her was about the last thing she wanted to think about. It had already taken her the better part of the week to erase that last horrible scene from her mind. She didn't know what had possessed her to make such a humiliating spectacle of herself. Although she had to admit, the stunned look on his face had almost made it worth it. Too bad the kiss had been so brief. It hardly even counted.

She folded the newspaper she was reading and stared thoughtfully at one article. "First National is offering eight percent loans."

Zoey waited until her mouthful of muffin became

more manageable then asked, "What kind of collateral are they looking for?"

Gracie's shoulders sagged. "Killjoy."

"Sorry, kiddo, didn't mean to rain on your parade, but you've got to be realistic about buying the boutique."

"I know. It's just that Martha is flying in tomorrow to go over the books and help with inventory, and I wanted to talk with her about moving forward with the buy-in."

Both women leaned back in their chairs while Darlene filled their coffee cups. The mall hadn't opened yet, and Cup-A-Chinos was dead. As much as she liked Darlene, Gracie hoped the woman wouldn't linger to talk. Right now, she needed Zoey's help in coming up with a plan to present to the boutique's owner. For all her faults, her friend was a fairly good businesswoman.

As soon as Darlene moved on, Zoey leaned forward. "Doesn't Martha want to retire yet? She's got to be pushing seventy. I'd think she'd be glad to get rid of it at this point. Maybe she'll give you some easy terms to assume any outstanding loans."

"Don't be too sure. You know how much she loves to travel, and all her buying trips are business write-offs."

"She still has the other two stores in Cleveland and Columbus."

Gracie propped an elbow on the table and let her chin sink into her palm. "She sold the Cleveland store two weeks ago."

"That supports my point. Sounds like she wants out."

"Not necessarily. This store is far more eclectic than the other two and requires exotic buying trips. Besides, I have a feeling she's been avoiding me."

Zoey snorted in disbelief. "Why would she do that? You're her best manager."

The door to the coffee bar opened, and both women automatically looked up. Adam strolled in, looking as surprised to see them as they were to see him. As far as Gracie knew, he hadn't been coming to Cup-A-Chinos since he'd moved into her place. She'd often wondered if he were trying to avoid her. It seemed he got home later and later from work each night. She'd only seen him one evening all week, and that had been a brief encounter.

He wore his customary jeans and white T-shirt, today with a green and blue flannel shirt and a Detroit Tigers baseball hat. As he approached, he lifted the cap, ran his fingers through his dark hair, then resettled the cap on his head. It wasn't a nervous gesture, exactly, but Gracie could tell he wasn't thrilled to run into them.

Zoey leaned way back in her chair, folded her arms across her chest and gave him the once-over. Finally, her gaze rested atop his navy blue hat, and she cocked her head in a manner Gracie unfortunately knew all too well.

"Bad hair day?" Zoey pleasantly asked Adam.

"Yeah," he said with a straight face, then winked at Gracie.

"I'm sure I have an opening this morning," Zoey said without missing a beat. "Why don't you stop by the salon?"

He gave her a dry look. "Why didn't I think of that?"

Gracie sighed. She didn't know what the problem was with these two. They barely knew each other, yet the tension between them was thicker than two-day-old espresso.

"Do you have time to sit with us?" Gracie asked, wondering how stupid this was. Allowing two bulls in the same arena. She slid Zoey a meaningful look.

Her friend straightened, a shrewd gleam entering her eyes, and Gracie was instantly sorry she'd issued the invitation.

"Yeah, Adam." Zoey pushed out a chair with her pointy black patent leather boot. "Get a load off. We could use some advice here."

He didn't want to sit with them. That was clear by the way he hesitated, his hands tucked into his back pockets, his lips pursed in indecision. And that was fine with Gracie, as her gaze followed Zoey's to the newspaper she'd been reading. She realized what her dear, pain-in-the-butt friend was up to.

Adam glanced at the wall clock, then took the chair Zoey had offered. "Always happy to be of service," he said, and signaled Darlene for some coffee.

"Gracie has this problem, and we want your opinion," Zoey began, and Gracie groaned.

"The key words are it's *Gracie's* problem," Gracie said with a forced smile. "Adam isn't interested."

"Well, you never know. He might be of some help." Zoey was all wide-eyed innocence, but she didn't fool Gracie for a minute.

It was fairly obvious what she was up to. She wanted to embarrass Adam. He wouldn't know anything about small business loans. He probably didn't even have a checking account. He wasn't going to be of any help. And Zoey knew it.

"I don't want to discuss this," Gracie said firmly.

A concerned frown drew Adam's eyebrows together. "Okay, we'll drop it. Whatever it is."

"For heaven's sake, Gracie Louise, he knows you want to buy the boutique, doesn't he?" Zoey quickly turned to Adam. "She's trying to find financing and talk the owner into selling."

"Zoey." Gracie drawled her warning as Adam shifted uncomfortably.

"The problem is, she doesn't have collateral," Zoey said. "Have any suggestions?"

He blinked, then looked idly to the right as if searching for something to say. Gracie was ready to splash her coffee across Zoey's lap to keep her from opening her big mouth again when Adam said, "You don't necessarily need it."

She transferred her gaze from Zoey to his wary face. There was a certain authority in the way he'd spoken that single sentence, and in spite of herself she asked, "What do you mean?"

"How long have you worked at that store?"

"Almost ten years."

"As manager?"

"For eight out of the ten."

"How much responsibility have you shouldered?" His face had taken on a serious look as if his thoughts were a jump ahead of his words. "You're not just a figurehead, are you?"

Even Zoey had straightened and was listening intently to what he was saying. She laughed at his last question. "Are you kidding? That old bat Martha never knows what's going on. She does everything Gracie tells her to do."

"Martha's the owner?"

Gracie nodded. "She's pretty hands-off. She does the buying, and that's about it."

"So, what are you getting at?" Zoey asked, starting to drum her long orange nails on the table.

"Many times banks are willing to lend money based on the new owner's experience. You take some of these large leveraged buyouts, for instance. When a group of upper-management people get together and buy a company, they generally don't have sufficient funds, but it's their expertise the lending institution is banking on to either make or keep the company profitable. Simply having money isn't going to turn the company's gears."

Frowning thoughtfully, Zoey stopped drumming. "I guess that makes sense."

"You'd be surprised how many successful businesses started out undercapitalized."

Gracie didn't say a word. She wasn't shocked, exactly, that he was so knowledgeable, but his undeniable confidence did surprise her. And made her wonder how he could be so content drifting from one menial job to the next when he was obviously capable of so much more.

"Tell me more about the owner, Gracie," he said, his tone cautious. "A lot can depend on her, as well."

It slowly dawned on Gracie why he was so hesitant. It wasn't due to lack of knowledge. She had told Zoey to drop the subject, and now he was worried about imposing or offending her.

She smiled her reassurance. "She doesn't really want to sell. And I can't blame her. Everything runs smoothly, and we've consistently turned a profit for the past six years."

"Does she know you want to buy the place?"

"I've told her I'd like first right of refusal if she ever plans on selling."

"And she was noncommittal?" he guessed.

Gracie nodded. "But her kids are trying to talk her into moving permanently to Florida. I think the timing's right for another shot at it."

Adam brought his elbow up to rest on the table and rubbed his jaw. Frowning slightly, he asked, "How good are you at bluffing?"

Even as Zoey started to laugh, Gracie felt her cheeks pinken thinking about the night Zoey, Brian and Dwight had tried to teach her to play poker. "Not very, I guess. What did you have in mind?"

"If this Martha thought you were willing to quit, which would mean more work for her, she might think twice about hanging on to the place."

Gracie let out a soft sound of exasperation. "I can't threaten to quit."

"Why not?"

"Yeah." Zoey perked up. "Why not?"

Gracie stared at the two of them in disbelief. "Because I need my job."

"And Martha needs you." Zoey waved an excited hand. "Adam's absolutely right. If she still refuses to sell to you outright, maybe she'll at least make you a partner." Looking extraordinarily pleased, Zoey glanced at Adam. "What the hell are you doing wasting away at a construction site?"

Adam's jaw tightened. Zoey's blunt question had irritated him, although Gracie could tell he was trying not to show it. He directed his attention at Gracie. "You can let her know how serious you are without jeopardizing your job."

"I don't know. She's kind of a peculiar lady."

"Is there anyone else who's qualified to take your place?"

"Not really."

"Would Martha be willing to step in?"

Gracie laughed. "She whines when I want to take only a week's vacation."

"Sounds like you're holding most of the cards."

Gracie worried her bottom lip. It wasn't that she didn't appreciate their advice and support, but neither Zoey nor Adam understood her position. Zoey was tough and assertive, and she could pull off a bluff. And Adam—well, longevity obviously wasn't his strong suite.

"Maybe I ought to worry about getting the financing first," she finally said.

Adam smiled. "You won't have any trouble. I'm guessing you've been dealing with the same bank for a long time now. Go to them. They know how dependable and trustworthy and capable you are. You'd be a winning endorsement."

"How would they know that?"

"This isn't that big a town, Gracie, and anybody that knows you at all surely knows that about you."

Her gaze flicked to Zoey, who was staring at Adam, her head cocked, the beginning of a begrudging smile tugging at her lips.

Gracie switched her gaze to him. "Thank you, Adam."

He grinned. "Just the facts, ma'am. Now, when are you going to make your move?"

"Well, Martha's coming in tomorrow night, and she's staying for a couple of days. I'll try to make an appointment with the bank for this afternoon or tomorrow morning."

He chucked her under the chin. "Don't take no for an answer, and don't forget, you're doing that bank a big favor." He pushed back from the table and started to stand. "If you're not doing anything tonight, I should be home early. We can go over your strategy if you like."

"I'll be there."

"I'll make dinner. Any requests?"

"We could just get take-out," she suggested.

His eyes crinkled at the corners. "Don't you trust me?"

She grinned, happy that their easy camaraderie had been restored. "Should I?"

He grunted something that was a cross between disgust and a sigh. "Probably not, Gracie, probably not."

Chapter Eleven

The steaks hissed and sizzled on the grill, and the potatoes had only ten minutes left to bake by the time Gracie got home. It had been dark for nearly an hour already, and Adam had had to change both burned-out patio floodlights to use the outside gas grill.

This wasn't the first area requiring attention he'd discovered in the week he'd been staying here. But it was by far the easiest to remedy. He was going to have his work cut out for him when the mall job was done. *If* it ever got done, he thought morosely, then shrugged away the guilt of having ducked out early today. This was the first time in over a week he'd gotten home before ten. Most of the men were still at the site.

Gracie parked her aged Nissan in the detached garage, hurried the short distance to the house and stopped to stare at him in surprise. He was huddled over the grill, freezing his butt off, about to flip the steaks for the last time. He'd tossed two ears of corn also on the fire, but he was about to give up and finish them in the oven.

"Do you know what the temperature is?" she asked, laughing.

"It doesn't matter. I shot past numb ten minutes ago." He lowered the lid and ran to the door as if it were the last out, last inning and he was stealing home.

Gracie crossed the threshold seconds before he came barreling in, and she stepped back to let him pass. Warmth and sweetness radiated from her, and he lingered near her heat long enough to remind himself why he'd stayed away all week.

She was getting to him. And neither one of them could afford to let that happen. He wasn't going to be sticking around. Gracie needed someone who would.

When he started to move away, she reached out and ran a warm palm up his cold, bare arm, her fingers stopping just short of his T-shirt sleeve. "Most normal people would have put on a jacket."

"Ah. I'll have to work on normal. Maybe Zoey can give me pointers."

"Hey." She lightly punched his arm. "I'll have you know she didn't make a single crack after you left today. In fact, she was pretty darned impressed with what you'd said."

He grabbed her fist when she started to withdraw it. "Not bad for a college dropout, huh?" He hadn't meant to sound so cynical, but she didn't seem to notice as she splayed her fingers and again let her palm cup his arm. Grabbing her wrist and moving it up and down so her hand created a pleasant friction against his skin, he said, "Come on, Gracie, warm me up."

"You should have worn a jacket," she told him, her voice a little breathless. She slanted her head to look at him, and his blood surged at how smoky her eyes had grown.

Odd, but he'd come to know her face so well in the three short weeks since he'd met her. He knew the exact moment her cheeks would begin to pinken in any given situation, and the way the corners of her mouth permanently tilted up as though always poised for a smile. Her lips were full, too, and soft-looking, and they colored right along with the rest of her face when she was embarrassed or uncomfortable.

He knew her eyes, too. They weren't distinctive in color or shape, but if he were put to a test and had to find them out of a hundred pairs, he'd bet his last dollar he could. Because they were kind eyes. They expected the best out of people, but if anyone fell short, he'd bet his soul those eyes would show tolerance.

Forcing himself to break the dangerous spell her rapt gaze was casting, he glanced at her coat.

It was navy blue, functional and shapeless, and it made him smile. His thoughts strayed to that evening in the basement, and he wondered what she was wearing under that ugly blue tent.

He cleared his throat and stepped back. "Dinner will be ready within fifteen minutes. What about you?"

"Sure. I'll be ready." She moved away and started to shrug out of her coat. "I just need to change."

Torn between helping her and getting the hell out of here as fast as he could, Adam rammed a hand through his hair.

One slim shoulder appeared. Most of it was covered by a gray sweater, but a large wedge of skin was bare. As the coat slipped down her arm, the snagged sweater went with it, exposing a thin lacy black strap molding her creamy white shoulder.

"I better check the grill," he said, and did an about-face.

"Wear a jacket—"

Her voice was interrupted by the slamming of the door as Adam raced into the brisk night air. It wasn't a cold shower, but it was going to have to do. No way in hell was he going to let his short-circuited hormones get the best of him. Gracie was off-limits. Period. End of story.

Besides, if the poor woman knew what he had on his mind half the time, she'd probably kick him and his swelling hormones out.

SHE WAS GOING TO have to seduce him. There was no other way around the problem that Gracie could see, she decided as she stared at the clothes in her closet. As much as she'd tried to ignore the strange images of him that popped up at the oddest times during the day or the frighteningly real dreams that had her breaking out in cold sweats in the middle of the night, she just couldn't shake her obsession.

She had to be realistic about this, she thought as she flipped through the row of pathetically unsuitable dresses and blouses. She could almost consider her condition a medical one. According to the magazines, it hit all women at a certain age. And she was tired of fighting it. Adam was going to have to understand, that's all.

Sighing, she pulled out a long-sleeved blouse. Turning it from front to back to front again, she frowned. Nothing to give him a hot flash over, but it *was* red, and it did have a vee. Shaking her head, she crammed the garment in with all the other disgustingly conservative pieces.

If she'd been operating with a full deck, she would have wisely brought home something appropriate to wear from the boutique. But lately, she was lucky to be able to keep her mind on the barest task. Today, when she'd been showing her favorite customer a pair of earrings, she'd called her Mrs. Adam by mistake. And then, after she'd taken the woman's credit card, she had to get the approval code three times from the charge company. These days everyone was looking at her strangely—her assistant, customers, the waitresses at Cup-A-Chinos. There was no question about it. She had to do something.

And tonight was definitely the night. If she didn't finally get him out of her system, how could she hope to have a fruitful conversation tomorrow with either the bank or Martha?

Grabbing an armload of clothes, she stumbled to the bed and threw the heap of blues and grays and browns across the quilt. Then she returned to the closet and repeated the process. By the time she got to the back wall, she still hadn't found anything eye-catching.

Hopeless. She was truly hopeless, she decided as she yanked off her dull gray sweater. Her navy flannel skirt followed. She resigned herself to wearing the new rust-colored tunic again. It wasn't anything spectacular, nothing that would light a fire under Adam, but it was new and it did have some color. It was going to have to do.

Her fanny hit the bed, and she started rolling down her panty hose. Then inspiration struck. She straightened and, in the dresser mirror, she stared herself in the eyes. She knew just the thing to wear. If she had the nerve to do it...

ADAM OPENED the oven door and poked the potatoes. In another three minutes, they were going to be more mashed than baked, and the corn was going to be creamed. At least he'd turned the heat off five minutes ago.

One of the many things he liked about Gracie was that she was a no-muss-no-fuss kind of a gal. He couldn't imagine what was keeping her, but she'd been upstairs for almost twenty minutes.

He'd just thought about knocking on her bedroom door when he heard the stairs creak—something else he'd added to his list of repairs.

The table had already been set and a bottle of Cabernet opened. Although he'd heated two dinner plates, they were now barely warm, and he gave up on them in favor of getting the overheated food on the table.

"Did I take too long?" Gracie asked from the doorway of the kitchen.

"You're just in time." Smiling, Adam looked up from studying a jar of mushroom gravy. If the steaks had gotten too well done, he had figured it would help. His smile faltered when he saw her. "Why are you wearing *that?*"

"This?" Her gaze fell from his face to the tan

trench coat, and she plucked at the too-wide lapels. Her eyelids had color on them.

"Are you going somewhere?"

"No." She shook her head and hurried into the kitchen to fill a water glass. "No. I thought it might be a little cold. Do you need some help?"

"Everything is ready. There's water on the table. And wine." He frowned at the tan monstrosity. It was so huge, it looked like a man's coat, yet it wasn't very cold in here. In fact, it was slightly warm. "Maybe I should make some coffee."

"I'll do that."

"Better yet, why don't we turn up the heat?"

"Oh, I don't think we need to do that," she said, color flooding her face before she turned away and started fussing with a glass pasta canister on the counter.

Adam rolled a stiff shoulder. He was missing something here, he thought. He stared at her back. His gaze traveled to the belt that cinched her narrow waist, to the well-hidden swell of her hips, to her bare feet. He stopped. *Bare feet?* Pink-tipped toes curled and dug into the yellow linoleum.

The oven timer dinged. They both jumped.

She didn't turn. She kept doing whatever it was she was doing while he continued to stare at her back. Her hair didn't seem any different. It looked pretty much the way it always did—soft and kind of tousled, not stiff or precise like the styles so many young women preferred.

He sniffed the air. Her perfume was a little heavier than usual. Something floral. It was hard to tell with all the food aromas.

"Aren't you going to get that?" she finally asked, darting a nervous glance over her shoulder. "You know...the buzzer."

"Uh, there's really nothing in the oven. I mean, there is, but the oven isn't on. I was using the timer for something else."

"Oh." She moistened her lips and started to face the counter again, but her gaze wandered past him. "For that?"

Before he had swiveled all the way around, he saw the smoke pouring out of the toaster oven. He bit off a curse and dived for it. But the chrome was hot to the touch, and he ended up letting the word fly.

Pulling a pot holder from a drawer, Gracie came to his rescue. She yanked out the tray of corn muffins. More smoke billowed out. Coughing and sputtering, she turned on the air vent over the oven. The air cleared quickly.

Adam stood there like a big sap, wondering what had happened. He scowled at the browned, crispy muffins. One minute he had everything under control, and the next he was burning Gracie's kitchen down.

"A little butter and we'll never know the difference," she said, and flipped one of the little suckers over. The bottom was hopeless. It was black and shiny. She pursed her lips. "This is my fault. I'm sorry I took so long upstairs."

"No, it isn't. I wasn't paying attention." He took the pot holder from her. "Go sit down. I'll bring out the rest of the food."

"Can't I help?"

He held up a hand. "How about if you pour the wine?"

She didn't argue, as if she could sense that he was suddenly strung tight. He didn't know what was happening. The nice pleasant evening he'd planned might just as well have gone with the smoke. Although burning the muffins had little to do with his tense mood.

It was Gracie who was getting to him.

And her damn pink toenails.

"Can I take your coat now?" he asked out of the blue.

She'd made it to the dining room table. Her hand slipped on the wine bottle. He closed his eyes, but opened them again when he didn't hear a crash. "I'm fine. Thanks," she said and picked up the Cabernet.

He dished up their plates and carried the sorry-looking meal to the table. The steaks were shriveled, the potatoes two giant lumps, and the corn, well, he wasn't sure even a bird could pick the dried-out kernels off the ears.

He set the plates down and said, "We're going out to eat."

She laughed. "What?"

"I screwed up dinner."

Her gaze rested heavily on the two plates. To her credit, not even a flicker of surprise registered on her face. "The potatoes are exactly the way I like them," she said calmly, "and I'm sure the steak is fine."

"Yeah, right. Come on, Gracie. You're already dressed." He pulled a jacket off the peg by the kitchen door. "We won't go any place far or fancy." Her eyes widened to the size of world globes, and he added, "Unless you want to."

"I'm not going anywhere." She abruptly sat,

picked up the glass of wine she'd poured and took a big sip.

Under the light of the chandelier, he could see the subtle colors on Gracie's face. Adam squinted. Her eyelids were sort of purplish, and her lashes blacker than normal.

"What's wrong?" she asked, squinting at him. "Why are you looking at me like that?"

"For a minute I thought I'd given you a shiner back there in the kitchen."

Her head tilted in confusion.

"You know, this." He pointed to one of his eyelids and grinned.

"I don't get it—" she started to say. Then comprehension dawned, and her eyes widened in exasperation. "It doesn't look like a shiner."

"You're right. My mistake. Let's go. Rosey's Steakhouse isn't too far. Ever been there?"

She picked up her knife and fork. "I have a perfectly good steak sitting in front of me. Would you mind getting the butter and sour cream while you're up?"

"Look, Gracie, here you are all decked out and everything. Let's just go out."

"I am not all decked out. I don't look any different than I did when I came home from work. You just didn't notice."

Adam didn't think that was accurate, but he kept his mouth shut. Maybe that's what was wrong. He hadn't noticed something earlier that he should have.

He hung his jacket, then brought the butter and sour cream.

"Thank you." She scooped a heaping spoonful of

each onto her potato. She didn't touch the corn. He didn't blame her.

As soon as he sat down, he remembered the mushroom gravy. "Look, if the steak's too dry—"

"Adam? Shut up and eat."

"Yes, ma'am." Grinning, he scooted his chair closer to the table. This felt uncomfortably like a first date. Like in high school. Except this wasn't a date. This was Gracie. "Do you want to go over your plan while we eat?"

She coughed once. Twice. "My plan?"

"Hey, we can wait until later when you're more relaxed. We might even want to save it for dessert."

She didn't have to look so shocked. He knew how to make pretty damn good brownies. From a mix. But not today. He'd only had time to stop at the bakery.

"What plan are we talking about?" she asked and grabbed her wine.

Frowning, Adam buttered his potato. "To buy the shop."

"Oh." She smiled. "Of course…after dinner would be good." She shook her head. "Or now. Now might be better. We might be too busy after dinner."

"For you, Gracie, I have all night."

Her grin faded a little. "I hope it won't take that long."

"What won't take that long?"

"Never mind." She dug into her potato with relish.

He cut off a piece of steak and tasted it. It wasn't half bad, although he noticed she hadn't touched hers yet. "Have you come up with any other plans since we talked this morning?"

Her gaze flew to his as she abandoned her fork. "What?"

"Hey, look what I'm doing. I said we'd talk business later, and here I am jumping in already. Eat."

"We can talk and eat," she said. "I have an appointment at the bank first thing tomorrow morning."

"Good. Do you have a balance sheet ready for them?"

"Believe me, there's nothing to balance."

He didn't say anything. He picked up the wine and filled their glasses, his expression thoughtful.

"That was a joke," she said. "I do have a few things to my name. This house, for one. Or at least the living room. The rest of the house is still mortgaged."

He smiled and hoped she'd hold on to her sense of humor. "I have something I want to discuss with you, and I want you to hear me out before jumping down my throat."

She took a sip of wine, her posture defensive suddenly, and he cursed himself for having set them both up this way.

He waited until she settled in her chair and said, "I have some money—"

Gracie shot forward in her seat. She started to hold up a silencing hand, but her little finger caught the lip of her plate. As she tried to free herself, the stoneware clanged against her wineglass, causing it to topple, the burgundy liquid streaming to the edge of the table and cascading onto her tan coat.

She started to get up, and he yelled, "Don't move."

A look of uncertainty flashed across her face, but

she settled back stiffly, looking helplessly at him, a ruby puddle in the middle of her lap.

"You don't want it to get on the carpet," he said as he set the empty glass upright. "Stay put, and I'll get some paper towels."

He didn't wait for her reaction. He rushed to the kitchen and ransacked the cupboard until he found a stack of paper napkins. When he returned to the dining room, she was exactly as he'd left her, her hands bunching up the fabric of her coat, her face nearly as red as the fist-size pond she was trying to keep pooled.

There were only a couple of small drops on the carpet that he could see, and after quickly blotting them, he pressed several layers of napkins onto the wine in her lap.

"I'll do that," she said, but when she let go of her coat, the wine dribbled toward a button and disappeared into the flap. Another wayward trickle headed toward the hem, and she quickly bunched up the fabric again.

Adam slapped napkins on both spills and stopped them from going any farther. Concerned that she not ruin the clothes underneath the coat, he stuck a napkin under the overlap.

She jumped, causing a wad of napkins to fall to the floor. When she bent to pick them up, her coat gaped, and he caught a glimpse of bare thigh.

He blinked. He had imagined that. It was freezing outside. She wouldn't be wearing shorts.

Or nothing.

His heart did a back flip. Would she?

He inhaled deeply. "I hope whatever you're wearing under that thing didn't get ruined," he said casually, and removed the rest of the soggy napkins from her lap. The puddle was gone. Only an ugly red stain was left. "There. This won't run anymore. Take the coat off, and we'll make sure your clothes didn't get ruined."

"It's okay." She held the front of her coat in a death grip that told him all he needed to know. "It's red...what I'm wearing...underneath. A stain won't show."

Adam swallowed, his pulse taking an erratic leap. If he had any lingering doubt as to what she was wearing—or not wearing—under that coat, the nervous jag in her tone confirmed his suspicion. More important, it told him he wasn't in this attraction alone.

He sucked in a dizzying breath. A gentleman would let her weasel out of the situation gracefully. Something he proudly considered himself ninety-nine percent of the time. But he wasn't a damn saint.

"Take off the coat, Gracie," he said. "It's best to deal with these situations right away."

Abruptly she stood, nearly sending her half-filled plate the way of the spilled wine. "I'll go upstairs and change."

He gently grabbed one of her wrists and pulled her toward him. She resisted at first, then inched closer, her head tilting back, her gaze slowly rising to meet his.

When only a heartbeat separated them, he slipped his arms around her and pulled her against him. Her hands flattened against his chest, her fingers flexed and uncertain.

"I've been wanting to do this for a long time, Gracie," he said softly, and touched the tip of his tongue to one corner of her mouth.

Her eyes drifted closed, a small, breathy sigh whispering from her lips and caressing his chin, before his mouth covered hers.

She pressed her palms against his chest, and for a moment he thought she was pushing him away. But her hands slid to his shoulders and cupped them, urging him closer, and he deepened the kiss. Her body shuddered against his, and he felt fragment after fragment of his control begin to slip.

The days and weeks of anticipation didn't come close to the sweetness of kissing Gracie. She was warm and soft and totally giving. There was no pretense or holding back in the way she slid her hands from his shoulders to loop around his neck. The way her soft full breasts snuggled against his chest. And when she breathed his name in that short, raspy way that told him her control was as elusive as his, Adam was left without doubt that she was with him in both body and soul.

The heady thought of this woman wanting him sent a fresh surge of heat through his bloodstream, and he throbbed with a need so great he knew he had to stop or there'd be no turning back.

He swept her mouth with his tongue one last time, trying to capture her sweetness before breaking the kiss. When he finally pulled away, her heartfelt sigh nearly made him dive back in for seconds.

"Gracie?" His voice was hoarse, his breathing uneven.

Slowly, she opened her eyes. Dark and slumberous, they infused him with renewed desire. "I...I—"

"Me, too." He hugged her to him, briefly letting his eyes drift closed. "I guess this makes us a little more than friends."

"I suppose so," she said, and her voice sounded small as she remained snuggled against him, her cheek pressed to his chest.

"Any idea what we should do about it?" He lifted a hand to stroke her hair, but other than that, neither of them moved.

"I'm not sure."

"I know." He kissed the top of her head, sharing her uncertainty and cursing it at the same time. "Gracie?"

"Hmm?"

"What's under the coat?"

She started to straighten, but he kept his arms around her.

"I should go upstairs and change," she said.

"Don't I get a peek first?"

"You may get more of a peak than you're expecting." Her eyes widened. "I didn't really say that."

If she hadn't reacted the way she had, with a look of such stark shock on her face, he may have missed her meaning. Laughing, he said, "I'll hold you to that."

And then he slipped her top button from its hole.

Chapter Twelve

After all her scheming, all her self-directed pep talks, all her bravado, Gracie wasn't sure she was ready for this.

Oh, her body was ready. She felt hot and tight and liquid all at once. Yet her mouth had grown incredibly dry, and she wasn't sure she could swallow or speak.

She managed to move her right hand and block his attempt to free her next button. Her fingertips rested lightly on his knuckles, but that was enough to get him to stop.

He turned his hand over, and their palms met. Rich brown eyes bore into hers. "Did I read you wrong, Gracie?"

"No." She wanted to look away, but that wouldn't be fair. She held his gaze. "I was trying to…I wanted to seduce you."

A slow smile curved his mouth. "You do that by breathing."

She blinked, and he laced his fingers through hers, then kissed her knuckles before lowering their joined hands.

At first she thought he might be angry because of

the way his jaw tightened and flexed. But as their hands came to rest between them, she brushed the unmistakable hardness behind his fly, and her breath caught.

His jaw tensed, and his chest swelled with his quest for air. And she realized that anger wasn't the problem. He was battling for control. A control she wielded.

Suddenly she felt a little dizzy, and she leaned into him. Sensual power was as unfamiliar to her as the coarse hair that brushed her fingertips at the vee of his T-shirt. But she could get used to it.

"Do you want to go into the living room?" he asked, but she barely heard because his breath was mingling with hers and his arm had come around to hold her.

She looked at the too-bright chandelier, at the scattered remains of their dinner on the table. Only several feet away, the front window looked over the street. They might as well be in a fishbowl.

Shoving self-consciously at her hair, she moved away from him. "Maybe we ought to clear away this stuff."

"We could," he said, and she started to reach for her plate. "But that will only delay things."

Her hand froze above the table. "Things?"

"Between us."

"Nothing happened."

"Yet."

She picked up the plate. Her hand trembling, she hurried to the kitchen.

"I'm sorry I'm attracted to you. I'm sorry I wasn't up-front about it before I moved in," he said, following her. He set the wineglass and condiments on the counter, then stuffed his hands into his back pockets and blew out a stream of air. "I thought I had everything under control."

"No harm done," she said with a lift of one shoulder.

He gave her an amused look. "Don't look so flip. You're in the same boat, and not talking about it isn't going to make it go away."

"Me?"

"Let's see under the coat, sweetheart."

She automatically tugged the lapels closer and sniffed.

"I'm glad you're so lousy at the seduction thing, or I'd be in worse shape than I am."

Her mouth dropped open. "Lousy—"

He grinned. "You're as nervous as a turkey in November. Admit it."

That did it. She glanced at the closed kitchen curtain, then reached for the button he'd abandoned earlier.

"Gracie." His tone held warning and surprise as his gaze followed her nervous fingers. "You don't know what you're doing."

That was probably true. She slipped the button free.

"Gracie." His voice broke, while his eyes remained transfixed on her hand.

Lousy at this seduction thing, huh? Her fingertips probed the next button.

He passed a hand over his face and exhaled loudly. "Okay, I give."

She grinned, no longer feeling nervous. This was fun. "What?"

''You're a goddess, and I'll do anything you want.''

Her grin broadened. ''Okay.'' She flicked the button free, and one side of the coat flapped to expose her right collarbone. ''Do the dishes.''

''What?'' His stunned gaze met hers.

She laughed, then crooked her finger for him to come closer. As soon as he took the first step, a fresh rush of nervous energy shivered down her spine.

When he took the next step, his eyes darkening to a rich milk chocolate, she started wondering what in the heck she'd gotten herself into…and where to go from here.

Her hand wavered, and she idly brushed the sensitive skin around her collarbone while trying to decide her next action.

''Gracie,'' Adam said, his voice hoarse and raspy. ''Are we going upstairs?''

She blinked, and he must have sensed her hesitancy because he stopped. And although she could tell he wanted to touch her, he kept his hands at his sides.

There would be no turning back once they crossed the line. They would no longer be mere roommates. And maybe not even friends. So much was at risk.

''I'm a little confused, Adam,'' she said, and noticed that his gaze went briefly to the wedge of bare skin at the top of her coat. When his eyes again met hers, her exploring fingers felt the exposed strap of her red teddy.

In the instant his gaze touched hers, blatant desire transformed to sympathetic understanding, and she knew she was probably a fool not to accept everything this man had to offer.

"I know," he said, and opened his arms to her.

She wasn't quite sure what she was agreeing to, but she stepped into his embrace, confident of her trust in him.

He held her close, doing nothing other than giving her comfort and understanding.

"You're determined to make a saint out of me yet, aren't you?" His chuckle stirred her hair.

There was no mistaking his meaning. As close as their bodies were, she felt his hardness against her belly. Yet his hand moved in soft, nonthreatening strokes against her back.

"I don't mean to give you so many mixed signals," she said, and pressed her cheek against his chest.

"I've contributed my fair share."

"This would be such a big step, you know?"

"I do." Hugging her tighter, he rested his chin on top of her head. "Maybe we really should be doing the dishes."

She heard the smile in his voice, and her lips couldn't help but curve. "Probably."

"I'm sorry I screwed up dinner."

"What dinner?"

He laughed, the vibration in his chest caressing her cheek. "You mean after all the trouble I went through—"

Laughing, too, she angled away to shove at his chest. He pulled his head back, and she stared at him, suddenly amazed at how familiar he seemed to her. One side of his mouth always seemed to lift a fraction higher than the other, and as his amusement grew, the groove in his cheek deepened. His eyes, though, were

what she remembered most when she wasn't with
him. They were alive with good humor, yet warm
with understanding.

And when he looked at her, she never had a doubt
that he was listening to every word she said.

Gracie didn't have to worry about finding ways to
please him or thinking up witty things to say. She
didn't have to worry about losing out to a computer
game before dinner was even over. Adam was here
with her because he wanted to be. He had said she
held his attention by merely breathing.

The realization both startled and frightened her, and
her hand drooped against his chest. Breathing was no
longer a simple matter.

"Gracie? What's wrong?" Covering her hand with
his, Adam ducked his head to peer with concern into
her eyes.

His heart pounded against her palm, and she
blinked when she realized she'd been staring at him
through a fog. She blinked again, and the haze started
to lift.

There was no longer any question in her mind.
Adam Knight was a risk she had to take.

"Gracie, tell me to go to hell if you want, but
please say something." Anxious creases were etched
between his brows, and his heart kept slamming her
palm.

"Kiss me," she said.

The creases deepened as his eyes narrowed and he
slowly, lightly pressed his lips to her forehead.

"I know you can do better than that."

"Is this another one of those weird signals?"

He'd barely gotten the last word out when she

looped an arm around his neck and pulled him toward her. She'd obviously taken him by surprise, and their lips met clumsily. But he recovered, pressed his hand into the small of her back, slanted his mouth over hers and deepened the kiss.

Gracie swayed a little, and he held her more firmly, taking one last taste before swooping and lifting her off the floor. She shrieked in surprise, her body jerking, but he cradled her to his chest and carried her out of the kitchen.

"I can walk," she said, laughing, a little breathless, supremely excited.

"Where's your romantic streak, Gracie?" He stopped at the edge of the living room to shift her into a more secure position. The bottom corner of her coat flapped open to expose one bare thigh. She reached for the coat but he bumped her into the air, and she fumbled.

"Hey, you're going to drop me."

"You bet." Grinning, he headed toward the stairs. "In the middle of a nice, soft mattress."

All rational thought stalled as she concentrated on taking deep, even breaths. But her brain quickly kicked into gear when she remembered the disaster in which she'd left her room while trying to decide what to wear.

"Okay if we go to your room?" She smiled. "It's closer."

He smiled back and sped up, taking two steps at a time.

She briefly considered that she really should be worried he'd drop her. It couldn't be easy maneuver-

ing the weight of a grown woman upstairs, but this
was Adam. And she trusted him to keep her safe.

Unlike hers, his room was neat and orderly. The
only item out of place was a pair of jeans over the
back of a chair. Even his bed was made. Not all tidy
and perfectly tucked in, but the blue quilt had been
pulled up to the pillow shams, and most of the creases
had been smoothed out.

He entered the room and headed for the bed. It was
clear he planned to drop her on the mattress as he'd
warned.

"Wait a minute." She switched her gaze from the
bed to the sudden wariness on his face.

"Change of heart?" he asked softly as he lowered
her feet to the floor.

"I'm not letting you off that easily." She gained
her footing but let her palms rest against his chest. "I
wanted you to put me down."

His alarm started to ebb, although a modicum of
uncertainty remained. "You can still change your
mind."

"I know." She lowered her hands from his chest
to his waist and yanked the shirt free of his jeans.

His nostrils flared, and the tic in his jaw returned.
He let his hands drop to his sides as he waited for
her to make another move.

Without hesitation, she grabbed the hem of his shirt
and pulled it up. He lifted his arms to let her take off
his shirt.

She threw it toward the chair with the jeans. It fell
short by a foot, and she resisted the urge to go and
pick it up. Sudden hesitancy sent color rushing to her
face as she stared at Adam's muscled chest. She

snatched back the hands that had been so brave moments ago and gathered the coat at her throat.

The only other time she'd worn the red teddy for a man, she'd ended up in tears. And Dwight was no prize himself. This man was pretty damn near perfect. What in the hell was she thinking?

Adam smiled. He covered her hands with his, and after a light squeeze, he pried her fingers from the coat. Cool air painted her bare skin with a coat of goose bumps as he pushed the fabric aside and went to work on the next fastened button.

The backs of his fingers brushed her sensitive flesh as he continued the path of liberation. Within seconds, the last hurdle was mounted and the coat parted to hang heavily, fatefully at her sides.

His gaze slowly assessed the landscape, and he inhaled a sharp breath while she held hers. "God, Gracie, you've given me a new respect for aerobics."

When his eyes finally met hers, the swell of desire she saw there made her dizzy and her breath came out in a rush.

The muscle over his right nipple jumped, and he reflexively lifted a hand to rub the area. "Maybe I need to join the class, huh? I'm getting kind of soft."

She laughed even as she had trouble dragging her attention away from his nipple. "I can't believe you'd fish for a compliment."

He blinked in genuine surprise before his gaze returned to her parted coat and instantly darkened. "I'm going to let that slide since I have more important things to worry about." He took a step closer, leaving barely room for a goose bump between them. "Like when you're going to lose that sorry excuse for a coat.''

He pushed the fabric off her shoulders while nuzzling her neck and let the bulky garment tumble to the floor. His hands slid around her, pinning her arms to her body, and his palms traveled the curve of her back to mold the swell of her buttocks under the silky teddy.

His lips were warm and slightly moist against the skin behind her ear, his hot breath sending tiny delectable shivers to her nape and down her spine. The sensation was so physical, she wondered if he could feel the tingling as his hands continued to caress the small of her back.

When he finally pulled back, the blissfully appreciative look in his eyes erased any remaining doubt she had about herself.

''Red is definitely your color.'' One hand came up to toy with the strap of her teddy. He extended a finger to trail her jaw. ''As much as I like it, I can't wait for you to take it off.''

She put her hands on his chest. His skin was warm and smooth against her palm. A thicket of dark hair fanned out around her fingers.

''You'll have to get it off yourself,'' she said, feeling slightly heady with new confidence.

One corner of his mouth hiked up, slow and cocky, then he kissed her quick and hard. ''Do you have any candles up here?''

''In the bathroom.''

He kissed her again. ''I'll be right back.''

''Adam?''

He'd already pulled away. When he stopped to

look at her, his dark brows creasing, she could tell by his expression that he'd heard the doubt in her voice.

She smiled. "Hurry back."

"Are you kidding?" He flashed her a killer grin before disappearing through the door.

Gracie immediately sat on the edge of the bed. Her legs were wobbly. Her nervous system had short-circuited hours ago, and her skin was so flushed she wouldn't be surprised if she ended up with a bad case of sunburn.

But she was happy. Happier than she'd been in a long time. And she felt beautiful. Adam's eyes told her she was.

She caught her reflection in the dresser mirror and raised a hand to her face. Her cheeks were warm to the touch. No surprise there. What did startle her was how different she looked. Maybe it was the brightness of her eyes or the way her hair was tousled. Her hand moved to smooth the errant strands.

"Don't." Adam crossed the room in three strides and set down the candles. "You look beautiful. Don't change a thing. Don't ever change anything about yourself, Gracie." He took the errant hand and kissed it. "Promise me."

She nodded. She couldn't speak. Too many thoughts were knotting in her head, and old feelings were emerging and being squelched in record time. "Thank you," she finally said.

His eyebrows drew together in confusion but he didn't press her for an explanation. Instead, he kissed her hand again before he turned to light the candles. Once the three flames licked the silent air, he flicked off the overhead light.

But when he sat beside her on the bed, he still looked troubled, as if he'd been trying to analyze her remark. "I have something to tell you," he said, his shoulder brushing hers, his hand resting familiarly on her thigh. "I've been meaning to explain something to you."

She didn't like the sudden drop in his tone or the way confidence wavered in his eyes. She wasn't sure she wanted to hear what he had to say, but she had to.

"This won't have any bearing on us. Especially not at this point. I hope you'll see that." He picked up her hand and stroked the inside of her wrist, and she realized this wasn't anything he truly wanted to talk about, either, which made her all the more anxious.

"It's about Zoey," he said.

He paused, and giddy relief arrowed through her. "Zoey?"

"Yeah, and about how we first met."

"Adam?" Gracie laughed softly. "I do not want to talk about Zoey right now. She'll come around."

"Maybe, but you don't understand—"

"Yes, I do. She is my friend, and it's sweet that you're worried about what she thinks, but I don't live to please Zoey. You were right. She has no bearing on our relationship."

"Geez, Gracie, would you let me finish?"

"No." Leaning forward, she placed both hands on his shoulders, and unprepared for her weight, he fell back on the bed. When their lips met, he stopped trying to talk and slid his arms around her.

It was fun and exciting taking the aggressive role without fear of being rebuffed. Quite the contrary, when Adam groaned low in his throat, she felt a fresh infusion of power and anxiously reached for the snap of his jeans.

He didn't wait passively to see what she was doing. He slid down one strap of her teddy to bare a breast and palmed the nipple until she was achy and hard. Then his lips left hers to trail tiny kisses across her jaw, down her throat. Just above her breast, his tongue took over and forged a path to her eager nipple. He circled it twice before taking it in his mouth.

Her fingers dawdled over his snap as the sensation he elicited became too exquisite to bear. He suckled and swirled and blew until Gracie was certain she'd entered another earthly dimension. When he lowered the other strap and worshipped her other breast in the same way, with great certainty she understood that life was over for her as she'd known it.

It was almost embarrassing, how quickly heat had pooled between her thighs. Her entire body felt liquid, like a flow of molten lava, rushing toward some kind of release. She wanted him to fan the flame. She wanted him to douse it. She hoped she could keep from exploding.

"Gracie," he whispered, his voice so hoarse she barely heard him. "Let's get this off you."

To her amazement, he'd already pulled the teddy as far as her waist, and he eased her backward until she was lying down and skimmed her hips with the red silk. As the material glided over her thighs and calves, each inch of skin awoke to his touch until he pulled the fabric free of her body.

Starting at her ankles, he reversed the trek, running his palms over her. Her muscles tensed in response, and he smiled. When his hands lingered at her thighs, she leaned forward and went to work on his snap.

He didn't try to stop her, but he didn't help her, either. He merely watched her through hooded eyes darkened by anticipation.

When her hands fumbled, he said, "Don't be in such a hurry, honey, we have all night."

She'd been distracted by the increasing bulge below her fingers, but she ordered herself to slow down and concentrate even though the liquid feeling had reached her hands.

After another failed attempt, Adam bailed her out and finished undoing his zipper. But after that, he offered no help. He waited for her to roll the jeans down his hips while he watched her with an intensified gaze.

Even with so simple a chore, lingering nervousness caused her to accomplish the task with awkward perseverance. When she finally got the denim to a point where she could pull it free, he stopped her and slid something out of the pocket.

She saw the foil wrapping in his hand as she cast the jeans to the side, and she felt a little sheepish for having been so turned on that she'd forgotten something so basic. Adam hadn't, though, and when the horribly destructive desire to compare his experience to hers tried to worm its way into her mind, she quickly expelled it from her brain.

She knew all she needed to know about Adam. He was here because he wanted to be with her. To him, she wasn't lacking. She was simply Gracie. And he didn't want her to ever change.

She smiled at him, and then her gaze dropped to

where the jeans had been, and she sucked in as much air as she could. He was gorgeous…and very ready…for her.

"We don't need this quite yet," he said, and leaned over to deposit the condom on the nightstand.

"We don't?"

He grinned, and she wanted to kick herself for sounding so eager. Still partially reclining, he gathered her to him and they fell heavily onto the mattress, her body half covering his, his erection pressing against her hip.

"No, we don't," he assured her, and ran the tip of his tongue from her throat to her breast. His hands found their own amusement, kneading her buttock muscles and driving her slowly and thoroughly crazy with need.

She squeezed her thighs together, afraid she was going to lose control at any moment. The action made her hip caress his hardness, and he groaned.

He increased the pressure of his mouth on her breast, and when one of his hands slipped between her thighs and slid into her, it was her turn to moan.

Reaching for him, she grasped his warm shaft and stroked the length of it. It pulsed against her palm, and his breath grew hotter and more ragged over her nipple. She was incredibly wet and she wasn't sure how much longer she wanted to hold out or even could hold out. She stroked him more insistently.

"Gracie…I thought…we…weren't ready." The words came out haltingly, as if he were having trouble breathing.

She closed her eyes and drank in the exquisite sensations rippling through her body. "That's what *you* said."

When she opened her eyes again, he was watching her. He thrust two fingers harder while his thumb probed another secret.

And the explosion began.

Chapter Thirteen

Adam watched the shock, then unadulterated pleasure enter Gracie's face, and his male ego nearly burst with satisfaction. She whispered his name just before she threw her head to the side and her hips pulsed off the bed.

Watching her was almost as good as climaxing. Even though he was close to seriously hurting himself by implosion.

"I can't take any more," she whispered brokenly, and he wondered if she realized she was pressing herself into his hand. He thrust a little deeper with his fingers and felt her shudders increase before they subsided.

Her hand had slackened around him, something about which he vaguely had mixed feelings. He was barely able to hold on to his control as it was. But she had a killer stroke he was gravely missing, too.

Almost as if she'd read his mind, her grip tightened, and the old rhythm was quickly resumed. It was his turn to close his eyes, his fingers slackening inside her. She moved until the contact was broken between her thighs, then she angled herself into a position to exert just enough extra pressure that he knew he'd better get that condom on quickly.

While she continued her magic, he stretched toward the nightstand. She didn't miss a beat as he proceeded to unwrap their protection. When he was done, he passed it to her.

Her glassy look faded, and she met his gaze with startled eyes. "I've never done this before," she said, her grip loosening.

"Just roll it on."

"It might be faster if you do it."

"But more fun if you do."

She laughed. It was a small, self-conscious sound but she started to do as he'd requested. When she was finished she peered critically at her handiwork.

Adam didn't know if he was more frustrated or amused, and he hauled her toward him until she was sprawled across his chest.

"Did I do it right?" she asked, her eyes wide and curious as he shoved the hair from her face.

"Honey, you're doing everything right," he said and urged her thighs apart.

As soon as they were in a suitable position, he thrust up, entering her and earning a look of sheer astonishment from Gracie.

"Sit up," he said, and she did, without hesitation, so that he could look at her flawlessly formed breasts, the endearing curve of her generous mouth.

Slowly, she experimented, moving up and down, wiggling a little, searching for the perfect rhythm. He was harder than a granite boulder, but he gritted his teeth, struggling for control, knowing she needed this time to get used to their union.

When she seemed to find her stride and he thought she was ready, he began moving his hips, meeting her thrust for thrust. She whispered his name between tiny breathy sighs, her short, blunt nails digging into his chest.

When he couldn't hold off any longer, Adam quickly maneuvered her until she lay with her back to the bed and he plunged into her, losing himself in her sweetness and trust, somehow knowing that after tonight, he was going to be a different man.

Two of the candles had burned out when Adam awoke the second time. One wick remained stubbornly lit but cast not much more illumination than a night-light. The moon was full, though, and with the curtains only partially drawn, he could easily see Gracie's slumbering face.

She'd slept peacefully most of the night. At least when he wasn't nibbling her ear or bothering her in some other way, he thought, smiling. But she hadn't complained. In fact, he'd recently learned something else about Gracie. She had incredible enthusiasm.

He brushed a strand of hair off her cheek, and her nose twitched. It was tempting to wake her again, but she needed the rest. She had a big day ahead of her, meeting with a bank officer this morning and then her boss tonight. Adam wished he could do something for her. He had more than enough money to assure her success in buying the boutique. But he also understood her need for independence.

A strong gust of wind shook the large oak outside his window. A branch whacked the glass, causing

Gracie to stir and snuggle closer to him. Tightening his arm around her, he rested his chin atop her head.

Wind and cold had buffeted the town all week, and although they'd only gotten rain so far, sleet and ice could be just around the corner. The mall job was behind schedule by two weeks. The possibility that this might be the first job in his career he was unable to finish on time nagged at him when he stopped long enough to think about it. Which hadn't been often.

He'd been working killer hours. Ironically, he'd been doing that as much to keep away from Gracie as to make up time on the job site. As addicted as he was to the adrenaline rush he got from beating the odds, this time the job simply wasn't his primary concern.

Using his free hand to scrub at his eyes, he sighed silently. He should have told Gracie about Zoey and the deal they'd made that first day in Cup-A-Chinos.

It seemed silly now. Hell, it had seemed silly then, but the truth was, he *had* agreed to Zoey's plan, no matter how tentatively. And although he'd returned her money and the plan had never developed the way Zoey had intended, he had a feeling Gracie might have a few choice words about the covert arrangement.

He'd wanted to explain everything before they had made love, but she'd caught him off guard last night, and before he knew it, the timing was wrong. He hoped she understood later when he explained.

For now, he thought, gathering her still closer and letting his eyes drift shut, he sure could get used to this. Falling asleep with her in his arms and waking up next to her was an addiction he wasn't ready to fight.

"YOU HAD SEX with him, didn't you?

Gracie looked up from the application she was filling out and narrowed reproving eyes at Zoey. "No, I did not," she said, honestly. They hadn't had sex. That was too common a word to describe their fantastic evening. They'd made love. Glorious, magical love. "Not that it's any of your business."

Her friend lifted her chin and snorted in disbelief before picking up her coffee and taking a loud sip.

The waitress had wandered over to refill their cups, and Gracie waited for her to leave before she laid her pencil down and asked, "Why did you ask me that?"

Zoey smiled at someone who'd just entered Cup-A-Chinos and made a point of looking miffed when her gaze came back to Gracie. "That disgusting glow."

"Disgusting glow?"

"That's what I said."

"If I *were* glowing, I don't know how you could consider that disgusting. But as it happens, I'm excited about my meeting with Bob over at the bank this morning."

She picked up her pencil and made another check on the form. She hadn't lied. She was excited over the encouraging news she'd received. Adam had been right. The bank was willing to lend her a small amount in spite of her modest collateral. And they had been very interested in her considerable retail experience.

Zoey sniffed. "They haven't given you the money yet."

"Well, Miss Pessimistic, what side of the bed did you get out of this morning?"

Her friend frowned. "You're right. I'm sorry."

Gracie laid down her pencil again. Something was wrong. Zoey was usually her biggest cheerleader. "You want to talk about it?"

"Not really, but I don't have much choice." Zoey ran her finger around the rim of her cup, her gaze pinned to the action, and if Gracie didn't know better, she'd think her friend was having trouble looking her in the eyes.

"You know you can tell me anything."

"Right." Zoey half laughed, the sound full of irony, and the reluctance with which she met Gracie's gaze was obvious. "Are you sure you haven't slept with him?"

She sighed her impatience. "I thought we were going to talk about *you.*"

"We are. But this involves you."

"I'm listening."

"Remember the day you told me about Dwight moving out?"

Gracie covered her face with her hands and groaned. "If this is about Adam or Dwight, I don't want to hear it."

"Would you chill out? I'm trying to get something off my chest here."

"Look, Zoey, I've got to fill this application out, return it to the bank this morning, get ready for inventory and pick Martha up at the airport by four-thirty. If you have a personal problem you'd like to discuss, you know I'm here for you. But if this is about me in any way, forget it.''

Zoey stared at a spot near Gracie's left ear for so long Gracie couldn't help but smooth the hair there. Finally, Zoey said, ''You're right. Now isn't the time.'' She lifted a shoulder and averted her gaze. ''It probably isn't that important, anyway.''

Gracie nodded, relatively sure of two things. Zoey's burning desire to talk had nothing to do with anything personal regarding Zoey or Brian. It did, however, have to do with Dwight or Adam. And Gracie wasn't up to hearing her friend's nagging or lecturing. Especially if it had the least bit of negative tone concerning Adam.

Zoey was right about one thing. The glow. Gracie had felt it the moment she had awoken this morning, feeling Adam's arms tightly around her. She'd felt it when he brought her coffee while she soaked in the tub, the strong brew made just the way she liked it— with one spoonful of sugar. And she felt it now thinking about the bone-melting things he whispered in her ear last night.

''You're not going to get that application filled out sitting there with that sappy grin on your face,'' Zoey said, a suspicious gleam in her eye.

Gracie couldn't help being a little irritated with her friend, yet she understood her concern, too. After all, Gracie hadn't known Adam long, merely a few weeks. And if the situation were reversed, she'd probably be worried that Zoey was rushing into things.

Except Zoey didn't know the entire story. Adam hadn't made any promises. He'd made it clear in the beginning that he was in town only temporarily, but while he was here, he made Gracie feel special. He listened when she spoke, and he paid attention to the things she liked. And most of all, he made her feel attractive again.

It wasn't like she was in love with him and she'd get her heart broken when he left. She picked at the corner of the application form, folding it over, then unfolding it. Because she already knew he *was* leaving. They were just friends. That's all.

"Hey, easy." Zoey's hand covered hers to stop her from mangling the paper.

Gracie blinked and stared at her friend. "I'm happy, Zoey. Really happy. Be happy for me, too."

Zoey remained stubbornly quiet for almost a minute, her gaze earnestly searching Gracie's face. "Then what happened to the glow?" she finally asked.

STARING at her employer, Gracie barely managed to hang on to her temper. She counted silently to ten, took a deep breath, then asked, "Martha, didn't you lead me to believe that you would seriously consider my offer at some point?"

"You know, I think it's time I gave you a raise. How long has it been since your last one?" Martha's graying brows drew together, and her pale blue eyes clouded in thought. "It doesn't really matter, dear. You deserve another."

"This is not about a raise. You've already gotten rid of the Cleveland store. Now you tell me you're selling the Toledo store, but you won't consider selling me this one?"

"It's not that simple." Martha massaged her arthritic left hand, the blue veins prominent below her thinning skin. "I need to have something to dabble in. What else would I do if I didn't have at least one store?"

Gracie stacked the last four boxes of costume jewelry behind the register. She would finish the inventory tomorrow morning. She'd had enough of voodoo doll brooches and feather boas for the night. She'd had enough of double-talking employers too.

Martha's anxious gaze followed Gracie's progress toward the back of the store. Although they had done the bulk of the inventory during business hours, they had closed up shop an hour early, and no one was in the store. A half hour ago, Gracie had sent home the two part-time clerks who had been helping them in order to give herself a chance to talk with Martha.

Although she had warned her boss weeks ago of her intention to discuss buying the store, the woman had managed to avoid anything but neutral conversation all the way from the airport, and it made Gracie nervous.

She got as far as the leopard print jumpsuits and stopped to turn to her wary-faced employer. "Why not keep the Toledo store and sell me this one?"

From the bridge of her heavily powdered nose, Martha removed her reading glasses and let them dangle from the thin silver chain around her neck. "There's so much you don't understand. It really isn't as simple as it all sounds."

"Well, then talk to me. I'm not an unreasonable person."

"I know that." The older women laughed. "You're too sensible for your own good."

Gracie frowned, slightly annoyed at the implication. "Just because I don't wear this stuff doesn't mean I don't know what sells well. Anyway, if it's the buying trips you're worried about, that wouldn't be a problem. You could continue on as long as you want. I have no desire to spend all my time traveling."

Her thoughts automatically flew to Adam. But after a couple of months, he wouldn't be here, anyway, she reminded herself. The idea wasn't pleasant, but it was one she'd better get used to. Which made ownership of the store even more important. She didn't need missing him to occupy her time. What she did need was something constructive to tackle. She needed to move forward with her life. Letting it revolve around a man had been a foolish, youthful mistake she'd already made. She wasn't willing to go that route again.

"It isn't the buying trips. I'm getting too old to travel so much." Martha pressed her lips together and smoothed the side of her ever-present French twist. Her proud chin lifted, profiling a jaw that was remarkably firm for someone her age.

Gracie slid the woman another covert look while straightening a rack of cat suits. It was totally unlike Martha to refer to herself as too old for anything. She was usually as vain as a self-absorbed twenty-year-old. Although Gracie had to admit her boss did appear to have aged since she'd last seen her, only six months ago. Her shoulders stooped slightly, and earlier Gracie had consciously adjusted her stride from the car to the mall in order to accommodate the woman.

Gracie's heart softened. "Martha, you do understand that I'm not trying to buy the shop because I think you're too old to run it, don't you? I fully expected that you'd continue to act in the capacity of buyer if our deal went through.''

A tentative smile eased the tension from Martha's face. "It's not you, dear." She closed her mouth, then opened it again as if she had something else to say, but instead, she pursed her lips and shook her head. Finally, she said, "Let's make sure we take care of the paperwork to reflect your raise before we go to dinner. I want it in writing."

Gracie gave her a quizzical look. They had largely agreed on most things over the years. And whatever issues they hadn't agreed upon, they'd still managed to resolve between them. There had never been a reason to put anything in writing. "It's not about a raise, Martha. And unless you plan on discussing my possible ownership, I think I'll skip dinner."

Shock registered in Martha's face, and her hand fluttered to the small locket she wore near her throat. Although they hadn't made specific plans to have dinner, it had become a tradition to go for Chinese after each inventory.

But Gracie didn't feel like making small talk right now. She was angry with her boss for having misled her and for being so unreasonable about explaining what was going on.

From one of the metal rounders, she grabbed an off-the-shoulder sweater dress she'd had her eye on earlier. "You want to write a ticket up for me? Or will you trust me until tomorrow? I'd like to take this home tonight."

Martha stared at the green and black animal-print

dress, then she stared at Gracie. "That doesn't look like something you'd wear."

"Why? Because it doesn't have pushover written all over it?" Gracie bit her lip when she saw hurt darken the older woman's eyes. Although she was tired of being the good girl, avoiding conflict at all costs, Gracie didn't want to be cruel, either. Her voice softening, she said, "Martha, I'm sorry. I didn't—"

Heaving a weary sigh, her employer waved a silencing hand. "No, you're right. We can skip dinner. I'm actually not very hungry." A humorless smile curved her lips while the old determination Gracie knew so well suddenly lit Martha's eyes. "But we do need to talk."

ADAM HAD JUST dropped off the trash at the curb when Gracie pulled her Nissan into the drive. The sides were splattered with mud and road grime from all the crummy weather they'd been having, and he made a mental note to get the car washed tomorrow evening. Knowing Gracie, she planned on keeping the thing until it fell apart, which meant she needed to keep it free of road salt so it wouldn't rust out.

What she really needed was a new car. One that was more reliable, especially when the weather turned bad. He had to see what he could do about convincing her to let him buy her one. He didn't want to have to worry about her once he'd gone.

The thought left a strange, hollow feeling in his gut. He shook out his hands and stretched his neck from side to side like he did when he was preparing for a long run. But the strange tension that had plagued him on and off all day clung to him like snow to a tree.

Jogging the short distance up the driveway, he reached her car just as she flipped off the headlights. When she didn't get out right away, he opened her door. She obviously hadn't seen him, and she jumped in alarm.

"It's me," he said, ducking so she could see his face by the interior light.

"I didn't see you out there." She blew out a relieved breath and relaxed the hand at her throat. "What are you doing out in the cold?"

"Tomorrow's trash day." He inclined his head toward the large can he'd hauled to the curb, but his gaze stayed on her face. Something was wrong. She was pale, and tension lined her mouth.

"You didn't have to do that," she said and started to get out of the car.

Stepping back, he grinned. "Do we have little elves living in the basement I don't know about?"

She laughed softly. "Thanks."

Come here," he said, when she'd moved free of the car. "Let's start over."

He pulled her willing body into his arms, and after kissing her on the lips, he hugged her to him. "Hi, Gracie," he whispered in her ear. "I missed you today."

"Me, too," she said and sighed sweetly, the sound reverberating throughout his chest as she snuggled against him. "What time did you get home?"

"About a half hour ago."

"So late?" She pulled back to look at him. "Were you working all this time?"

He nodded, wanting her against his chest, sighing, telling him how much she missed him. "We're still behind schedule."

"Well, they work you way too hard."

Someone down the street banged the lid of a trash can, the sound echoing through the still night air, and she moved away to grab two bags and her purse from the passenger seat.

Adam chuckled. Ah, the romantic sounds of the suburbs. He took the packages, slipped an arm around her shoulders and steered them toward the back door. "How did it go?"

"I had dinner with Martha after we finished the inventory," she said, and by her defeatist tone he knew that was the source of her tension.

"I know. I got your message. That's part of the reason I decided to work late."

"Really?"

She was grinning in earnest as he pushed open the door. "Well, yeah. I knew you wouldn't be home, anyway," he said, not sure why or how he'd made her so happy, but damn glad he had.

She flipped on the light, set down her purse and started to shrug out of her coat. "Have you eaten?"

"I picked up some cashew chicken and moo-shu pork on the way home. I figured you'd do more talking than eating with Martha and you might still be hungry."

Laughing, she nodded toward one of the bags he'd carried in for her. "I guess we'll have plenty of leftovers for tomorrow."

He looked more closely at the logo on the bag.

"Chinese, too? See, Gracie, we have more in common than you think."

"I know," she said, quickly averting her face and busying herself with hanging up her coat.

He gave her a moment by putting the food away. He was actually pretty impressed with himself and the restraint he'd so far demonstrated. All day he'd thought about holding her, kissing her, making love to her. But he knew Gracie had more on her mind than playing spin the bottle with him.

But his patience and understanding only extended so far. And the woman was never going to make a saint out of him.

He moved behind her, circled an arm around her waist and hauled her against his tightening body. "Tell me about your day, Gracie," he said, while pressing light kisses down the side of her neck.

She giggled and squirmed, which did nothing for his lingering attempt at restraint. "How can I talk when you're doing *that?*" she said, shaking her hair to give him better access, and her entire body shimmied.

"Keep doing what you're doing, and we won't be talking."

The top of her fanny made a strategic rest stop, and he groaned in her ear. "Did you say something?" she whispered.

"You little witch." He gently bit her neck, his teeth making light tracks to her jaw.

"Is that supposed to discourage me?" Her voice was soft and breathless, and he was greatly torn between carrying her upstairs and finding out how her meeting went.

He made his decision just as the phone rang.

Gracie sighed loudly and let her head drop back on his shoulder. "Zoey," she said immediately. "Only she would call this late."

He wanted to tell her to let it ring, to let the answering machine pick it up, but by the fourth peal, she moved to get it, and he didn't stop her.

Instead, he started to leave the kitchen to give her privacy. When he heard her begin to relay the evening's events to Zoey, to his amazement, he found he was jealous. He wanted to be the one to share her problems, to help her find solutions. But he reminded himself that within a couple of months he'd be leaving. And that inescapable fact destroyed his right.

Chapter Fourteen

Gracie hung up the phone and went to find Adam. It was late, and she was tired, emotionally drained and in need of a big hug. She knew without a doubt that one was waiting for her.

He was sitting on the couch writing out a check when she found him. She frowned, although she shouldn't be suspicious. He had bills to pay like everyone else. She had no reason to assume the check had anything to do with her.

Still, it made her uneasy, and she wondered how much of her conversation with Zoey he'd overheard. Not that she planned on hiding anything from him. It wouldn't matter, anyway. The boutique simply wasn't for sale.

He looked up when he heard her weary sigh, and a smile instantly curved his mouth. "Come sit with me."

She approached the couch, but before she could slide in beside him, he snagged her wrist and pulled her on his lap.

For a moment she wanted to forget all about Martha and the store and all her disintegrating plans. She wanted to lead Adam upstairs, slip between warm, scented sheets and lose herself in his seductive love-making. Because she knew he would make her feel beautiful and wanted and everything she was still learning to be. But she also knew that Adam couldn't solve her problems. Besides, it was nice just having a friend right now.

"Comfortable?" he asked.

Snuggling so her head rested against his shoulder, she nodded. "I needed this."

"Can you tell me about it?"

"Martha can't sell the store."

"Can't or won't?"

"Both, sort of. Her family has gotten involved, and her granddaughter, who's just gotten out of college, will be taking over."

"Running the store?" He withdrew slightly as he tried to look at her.

"Not exactly, although she would become my new boss. She'd mainly be going on buying trips. It's a great way to write off vacations, and it seems her granddaughter wants to see the world." Her tone dipped with weariness, bitterness and disappointment, and she shrugged. "It's not Martha's fault."

"That sucks."

She chuckled. "I couldn't have said it better myself."

"From what you've said, I thought Martha had more backbone than that."

"She always has, but I think she's feeling her age. She doesn't want to make waves, because her daughter is pushing pretty hard for her to turn over the business and retire to Florida to be with the rest of them. Besides, Naomi has always been her favorite granddaughter.''

"Where does that leave you?''

"With a job, at least.''

"That's not good enough.''

She smiled in spite of how awful it felt to rethink the whole mess. He sounded ready to stand up in arms for her. Just like Zoey had.

"If it were any other obstacle I would fight tooth and nail, but I don't want to place Martha in a difficult position with her family. I'll just have to go to plan B," she said, and started tracing small circles on his chest with the tip of her finger.

"What's plan B?''

Raising her gaze to his, she made a face. "I haven't figured that out yet.''

He frowned as if deep in thought, then narrowed his eyes. "I'm assuming the store has been making good money since the bank was willing to take a chance on you.''

"We've made record profits from the month after I took over as manager. I'm sure that's the main reason I'll still have a job. Her family wouldn't know me from a perfect stranger.''

"You can use that to your advantage. Tell Martha that you're seriously thinking of resigning. Bluff a little. If her granddaughter thinks—''

"Adam," Gracie said softly, and he stopped talking. She hesitated, trying to think of a polite way to tell him to shut up. "I appreciate the fact that you want to help." The defenses he obviously raised immediately darkened his eyes. "But I need to work this out myself.''

She couldn't tell if he looked more surprised or irritated, and she added, ''That's sort of the difference between men and women…in my experience, anyway,'' she hastened to include. ''Men always want to jump in, take over and fix everything. All I wanted was for someone to listen. I have to find my own solution. Do you understand?''

Surprise clearly won out over irritation, and he lifted a shoulder. ''Yeah, okay.'' And then, to her relief, he started laughing. ''You're right. All I could think about was fixing things for you.''

''And that's very nice. But all I want is a friend right now. Not a hero.''

An odd expression crossed his face as he appeared to consider what she'd just told him. Then one corner of his mouth lifted, and he said, ''You know how we've established how friends hug and do certain things?'' She nodded, and he added, ''Could we expand that to something else?''

''Absolutely,'' she said, smiling, and grabbed the front of this shirt.

When their hungry lips met, the kiss was anything but friendly.

ADAM TRANSFERRED his gaze from the blueprints to the date digits on his watch. He cursed under his breath. During the last three weeks, he'd worked everyone to their breaking point. The men hadn't complained, because the majority of them wouldn't have jobs for most of the winter months, and they stockpiled their overtime pay like squirrels hoarded acorns.

But he knew everyone was tired and starting to get

edgy, and despite their efforts, the job was still several days behind schedule.

He wasn't in much better shape than his men. Although Gracie was readying the store for the Christmas rush, she was arriving home at a reasonable hour each evening, and all he could think about most of the time was being there with her.

They had settled into a nice routine, taking turns either making dinner or bringing home take-out from the Chinese restaurant at the end of their street or from the Italian deli in the mall. Except that he was starting to get home later and later, and he didn't want her always having to wait for him.

But she never complained. Invariably she had a smile on her face as he came through the door each night, and it took only a matter of seconds before their kisses got so heated that dinner nearly became a moot point, anyway.

Even Zoey was coming around. She was usually civil to him, and their original deal seemed to be a dead issue. She never spoke of it, and it rarely crossed Adam's mind anymore. Occasionally he thought about telling Gracie. She'd probably get a laugh out of it at this point, but she was never around when he thought about it.

In fact, the main problem was, *he* didn't seem to be around much any more. A reality he was helpless to change. If he'd been determined to finish this project on time before, he was twice as motivated now. Meeting the deadline would give him just the bargaining tool he needed to get Gracie the store she wanted.

There was no question that he had to succeed. If

not for her sake, then for his own. Because if he made
certain she was well taken care of, then just maybe
he wouldn't feel like such a total heel when he had
to leave her.

GRACIE HUNG UP the phone and frowned. Adam's
mother didn't sound at all like someone she'd expected. Not that she'd had any expectations before
having heard the woman's cultured voice. In fact,
Adam didn't speak much about his family. Gracie
only knew that they all lived in Texas, although his
mother's southern accent was very slight.

It wasn't as though they had a lot of time to discuss
much of anything. Adam worked incredibly long
hours, and when he got home they chatted about the
day's events and other nonsensical topics over dinner.

As nice as it would be to have him around more,
she fully understood his desire to make money while
he could. Although he didn't talk about it, she figured
he might be worried about where he'd find his next
job. She hoped it was here in town. But he hadn't
made promises, and she was too chicken to ask.

She heard a noise at the door, and when she turned,
Adam was opening it.

He stamped his boots on the welcome mat just like
she'd seen him do dozens of times before, and the
sudden thought that he would be doing that for the
last time soon nearly made her double up in pain.

"What's the matter, Gracie?" He hurried over the
threshold and caught her in his arms. "You look
pale."

"Your mother called," she said, because it was the
first thing she could think of to say.

His face creased in a frown. "What did she say?"

"Nothing. I told her you weren't home yet."

Glints of anger sparked from his eyes, and it startled her, because he rarely displayed any temper. "She obviously said something to upset you."

"No. I'm not upset." Her shoulders lifted in a helpless gesture. "The only thing your mom said was that she wishes you'd quit sending checks."

His eyebrows drew together as he considered that information, and then an odd, satisfied smile tugged at his lips. "I'm surprised she told you that."

"I don't think she meant to. She seemed a little embarrassed, and then she just asked that you call her back tomorrow. We hung up right after, but that was only a few minutes ago. You could probably still catch her."

"Whatever it is, it'll wait until tomorrow." He pulled her possessively against him, just the way she liked him to, the way she'd become accustomed to in the past three weeks. "Now, tell me about your day."

She smiled at him, and his breath warmed her cheek. "Didn't you say your mom works at a university?"

"Yeah, why?"

"Stop that. How can I concentrate if you're blowing in my ear?" It was difficult to look stern when her toes were starting to curl. She swatted his arm, and he finally stopped, but not without giving her a devilish grin.

"Why did you want to know about my mother?"

She gave him a quick kiss, then broke contact or she'd bet her next paycheck they wouldn't get around to dinner. She opened the refrigerator door and got out the leftover meat loaf and scalloped potatoes they'd had last night.

"I don't know. She didn't sound like I thought she would."

"Her nose is usually so high in the air, her feet don't touch ground." He cut a sliver of cold meat loaf and popped it into his mouth. "It's hard to talk to people at that altitude."

He tucked plastic wrap around the sides and carried the plate to the microwave. After he set the timer to heat the food, he caught her stunned expression and laughed.

"What? Why are you looking at me like that?" He shrugged, taking the container of scalloped potatoes from her hands. "I didn't say anything I wouldn't have said in front of her."

"I'm sorry. I don't know what to say."

"I obviously gave you the wrong impression. We get along fine."

She studied his casual demeanor as he removed the lid and replaced it with plastic wrap, readying the dish for the microwave. There was no bitterness or anger in his expression. In fact, his face was totally blank...until he suddenly frowned.

"Damn. I meant to stop on the way home and pick up some Tabasco sauce," he said, and she let out a short huff of exasperation. "What?" He blinked at her.

Placing a hand on her hip, she tried to decide whether she wanted to admit to how curious she was about his relationship with his mother.

"Hey, the fact that I want Tabasco doesn't say

zilch about your meat loaf. I'm from Texas, remember. I like spicy food.''

"You turkey.'' She shook her head and opened the refrigerator door to get out the salad fixings. If he wasn't going to volunteer, she wasn't going to ask. And if he wanted to be deliberately obtuse, well...

"Does this have to do with my mother?'' he asked, his eyes narrowing.

"Does what have to do with your mother?''

He gave her a dry look.

"Okay, okay. I *am* curious.''

He pursed his lips and drew his eyebrows together as though he had to give the situation some thought. "When I was young, we constantly butted heads. I was always a disappointment to her and my father, but we've ironed out most of our differences over the past few years.''

Gracie's eyes widened. "How could you possibly have been a disappointment to them?''

A slow smile started to curve his mouth, and he pushed the dish of potatoes aside. "I dropped out of college. Almost everyone else in my family has a Ph.D., or at the very least a master's degree.''

She shrugged. She could understand a parent's *brief* disappointment. Anyway, Adam was...Adam. How could he disappoint anyone? "And?''

The microwave dinged, signaling that the meat loaf was ready, but he ignored it and stepped closer to her, his grin broadening.

"Uh, dinner is ready.'' Her gaze darted to the still cold potatoes. "Half of it, anyway.''

"Come here, Gracie Louise Allen.''

She tried to keep her answering smile at bay. "We were talking about your mother."

"I have a better subject that's come up."

Her gaze traveled down the front of his jeans, and she couldn't help the grin any longer. Nor could she do anything about the darn blush that stung her cheeks. "I take it back," she said, and belatedly realized she hadn't voiced her thoughts aloud. "You aren't so perfect, after all. You're incorrigible."

His right brow hiked up. "You think I'm perfect, huh?"

"Not anymore."

"Let's see what I can do about that." He slipped an arm around her waist, sending her pulse on a mission to the moon. And when his tongue slipped between her lips, Gracie gladly cried uncle.

ADAM YANKED off his hard hat and flung it onto the passenger seat of his truck along with the courier's message. They were finally making some decent progress at the job site and old man Carpenter wanted to have a meeting…in the middle of the day…as if Adam wasn't already busy enough, busting his butt to get the man's mall finished in time for the Christmas rush.

It had crossed Adam's mind not to respond so quickly, to make the guy wait until after dark when the first shift packed it in and it would be easier for Adam to get away. But he had something he needed to discuss with the developer, too, and he figured the sooner he got the new deal he wanted to propose off the ground, the better he'd feel.

Time was growing short.

At this point, with the overtime everyone had been putting in, he felt confident that the job would be completed within three weeks, which meant he'd meet his deadline. After that, he figured it would take him about a week to tackle the repairs around Gracie's house, maybe two weeks if he stretched out the work.

He didn't want to leave. The thought of stepping off her porch and kissing her for the last time burned a hole in his gut the size of Texas. But he had another job waiting for him in Alabama, and the sorry truth was, she hadn't asked him to stay.

They never talked about him leaving or how they'd keep in touch after he left. She hadn't brought the subject up even once. Maybe she didn't want to ruin the remaining time they had together.

Or maybe she didn't care for him as much as he did for her.

Now, there was a cheerful thought. Adam jammed the truck into gear and peeled out of the parking lot, kicking up enough dust to choke a small neighborhood. Stretching his tense neck from side to side, he eased up on the accelerator.

To be fair, he hadn't brought up the subject of leaving, either. He almost had once, about two weeks ago after they'd had dinner. But then Dwight had shown up, arguably to pick up some of the things he had stashed in the basement.

Adam knew better. The guy still had the hots for Gracie. Not that Adam could blame him. The poor slob was probably kicking himself for letting her get away. Gracie was the kindest, most giving, most non-judgmental person Adam knew.

He smiled. And she just happened to be gorgeous.

Luckily for him, Adam didn't believe Dwight's feelings were reciprocated by Gracie, but after Dwight's appearance that night, the mood to discuss any possible future for her and Adam had certainly been destroyed.

He'd never tried to bring the subject up again. The job kept him busy until nearly ten each night, and Gracie had taken on two more aerobics classes, trying to save enough money to find another store in the likely event that her final appeal to Martha's granddaughter fell on deaf ears.

He hoped his plan would spare Gracie the trouble.

At least then, when he left, he'd know she was okay.

The pathetic image of Dwight the last time Adam had seen him flashed in his mind as Adam steered into the parking lot of Carpenter Enterprises. Unease, pricklier than desert cactus, crawled up his spine, making Adam wonder if he were looking at himself several months from now. Like Dwight, was he going to be kicking himself for walking away from the best thing that had ever happened to him?

Thomas Carpenter pulled his late-model silver Mercedes into the reserved space alongside Adam's pickup. Sporting a fur-trimmed red parka and dark wool slacks, he hopped out of his car and approached Adam before Adam could climb out of his truck. His movements were swift and economical, especially for a man well into his seventies. When Adam got to be that age, he hoped he had the good sense to retire and take it easy for a change. Of course, he'd heard the guy had no family. Maybe the business was all he had to keep him going.

"Knight, glad you could make it so fast." The older man extended his hand, which Adam grasped while he slammed his truck door with his other hand.

"What's this about, Carpenter?" Adam got right to the point. The developer was a no-nonsense businessman, something Adam appreciated. "You know how tight we're running."

"That's what I want to discuss." Carpenter pulled up the fur collar of his jacket against the November chill, then gestured toward the entrance of his low-rise office building. "Let's walk and talk."

"I'm going to meet the deadline, if that's what you're worried about," Adam said, matching the man's brisk strides.

"Of course I'm worried. I didn't get rich waiting around for things to happen." He pushed open the glass doors, and they proceeded inside. "But I knew your reputation, son, and I'm betting you finish on time."

He paused to wave off his approaching secretary, then ushered Adam into his office and closed the door. Before he made it all the way around his massive walnut desk, he narrowed his steely blue eyes at Adam and said, "I need the job done faster."

Adam snorted. "You gotta be kidding."

"I never joke about business or money. What will it take?"

Adam slowly sank into one of the burgundy leather chairs opposite Carpenter's desk. This new snag could turn things in his favor. "How much faster?"

"A week earlier than what we'd originally agreed

upon," the older man said while shrugging out of his parka, his cagey eyes not missing a single nuance of Adam's reaction.

"A week, huh? All those new stores can't possibly be ready for Christmas in time."

"I've got my reason, Knight. Can you deliver or not?"

Adam traced the seam of his jeans while he bought time. It wouldn't hurt for the tycoon to stew for a minute or two. He was used to getting what he wanted when he wanted it. A little anxiety might make him more agreeable. He didn't need to know that Adam had already expected to finish a few days ahead of schedule. Making up the other days Adam would worry about later, even if it meant he worked nonstop.

"Yeah, I can do it. For a price."

"Of course."

"I want one of the stores."

"One of the empty ones you're just finishing?" The developer leaned back in his chair, his face creased in disbelief. "You can't be serious."

"We have something in common, Carpenter. I never joke about money or business."

"That isn't possible. I already have tenants lined up. Most of the contracts have been sighed."

"And I want a ten-year lease." Adam frowned. Gracie was going to have to initially put out a lot of capitol for inventory. "No, make that fifteen, rent-free for the first five years. We can establish a reasonable amount after that."

"Are you listening to me, son?"

"How badly do you want this project completed on time?"

"You mean a week early, don't you?" Carpenter asked, over steepled fingers, and when Adam didn't comment, the older man barked out a laugh. "I could accuse you of blackmail."

"You could."

A stony silence followed while Adam gauged his opponent and planned his next move, but before he could formulate a rebuttal, the other man said, "It's got to cost you more than meeting this new deadline. You're asking for too much."

"I'm listening."

"You have to give up the bonus I promised you."

"Done." Adam stood, ignoring Carpenter's look of stunned surprise. "Let's get this in writing. I'll leave that up to you."

The developer shook his head, a triumphant gleam entering his eyes. "Do you have any idea how much money you just flushed down the john?"

Wordlessly, Adam headed for the door. He knew he could have bargained, that he'd just let himself get screwed. But his heart wasn't in it. Because he knew that no matter what, he was going to be a loser the minute he stepped off Gracie's porch for the last time.

And no amount of money was going to change that.

GRACIE HEARD Adam's truck being parked in its spot alongside the house, and she quickly pulled the turquoise teddy from her drawer and slipped it on. She smiled, thinking how silly it was to be in such a hurry to get dressed when she knew he'd have her naked again in a matter of minutes.

But they'd gotten into a routine, of which she'd become quite fond. Besides, Adam always seemed to love finding out what kind of lingerie she was wearing under her clothes each day. And she found a great deal of pleasure in not disappointing him.

"Gracie?"

She hurried down the stairs to find him coming out of the dining room. His dark hair was so windblown she couldn't see the slight ridge his hard hat normally left. A day's growth of beard shadowed his strong jaw.

Her pulse leaped at the sight of him, just like it always did, just like she imagined it always would. At least for another month.

She felt her smile slip at the thought of him leaving and ruthlessly pushed it away. No promises, she reminded herself. That was part of their unspoken deal.

"You're home early," she said, and stepped into his arms.

He kissed her on the lips, then along her jaw, behind her ear. "I missed you."

She laughed, the sound a nervous rattle in her throat. He sounded so serious. "We met for lunch, remember?"

"That was a long time ago."

She pulled slightly away. "I stopped by this afternoon to see if you'd be home early enough to meet Zoey and Brian for dinner." Her eyes met his, and she saw the surprise reflected in their brown depths.

"You came to the job site?"

She nodded. "Is that a problem? I didn't get you in trouble, did I?"

"No, of course not." His arms fell to his sides. "I didn't get the message."

"I didn't leave one. They said you were at a meeting, and so I just left.'' She stared at the troubled look on his face and wondered what she'd done wrong. Although he'd said it wasn't a problem, she got the distinct impression that it wasn't okay for her to have gone to where he worked.

She'd never been there before, and she had been a little curious. When one of the guys told her he was in a meeting, her curiosity doubled. From the little of what she knew of Adam's job as a casual laborer, she couldn't imagine why he would be involved in any type of meeting.

Her nosiness must have showed because he said, ''The mall owner wants the job done a week earlier. He told us today.''

''Oh, no.'' She sighed, her shoulders sagging as she led him into the living room. ''You're working so hard as it is. They can't expect you to put in any more hours, can they?''

He laughed. ''Yeah, they can.''

''Not only is that unfair, it's unhealthy. There's got to be some kind of safety law preventing them from abusing you like this.''

His smile was pure indulgence as he sat on the couch, pulling her down beside him. ''We work in shifts. Anyway, most of the guys won't complain. They need the extra money. Once the temperature stays below freezing, jobs will get scarce.''

Pursing her lips, Gracie picked at a loose thread on the front of his blue flannel shirt. This was the perfect time to bring this up…if there was such a thing as the perfect time. ''I don't want you paying any more rent.''

He looked startled, then he looked angry, storm

clouds gathering fast and furious in his dark eyes, but she knew that was his ego responding, and she held up her hand when he opened his mouth to protest.

"You can pay me back later if you want, during the summer when you can find more work. Or you honestly don't have to pay me at all. And I know it's none of my business, but your mom doesn't need the money, and I hate to see you killing yourself so you can send her a check every two weeks."

He frowned, confusion blending with irritation. "How do you know she doesn't need the money?"

"She called again today. She said she hasn't cashed the last two and she won't cash anything else you send." Gracie traced the outline of a heart with her fingertip on his shirt sleeve, her eyebrows knitting together as her gaze met his. "She also said that a professor's salary isn't anything to sneeze at."

"She said that, huh?" He looked past her into space, a slow grin stretching across his face.

"I thought you said everything was okay between you two now?"

His attention shot to her. "It is."

"Then why do you keep taunting her and looking so damn proud of it?"

"I'm not taunting her."

His stunned look shook her confidence. Apart from the fact that she had no business delving into his private affairs, it looked as though she was off the mark. "I'm sorry," she said. "I shouldn't have said that."

"I'm not taunting her," he repeated, and when Gracie didn't respond, he rammed a hand through his hair and huffed in frustration.

"I just wanted to show her that I didn't need a

college education to make a success out of my life.''
He stared hard at Gracie before passing a hand over
his face and blowing into his palm. Impatiently, he
dropped it, and said, ''I'll quit sending the checks.''

She laid a hand on his arm. ''It wasn't my place
to interfere. I'm sorry. Whether you send the checks
or not is between you and your mother. But if you
think for one minute that you're not a success, I'm
going to bop you right in the nose.''

His eyes started to crinkle at the corners. ''Even if
I'm just a handyman?''

''That's what you do,'' she said quietly, ''that's not
who you are.'' When she leaned toward him, the last
thing she saw was a strange emotion flicker across his
face before their lips met.

Chapter Fifteen

The next morning, Gracie awoke before Adam and quietly slipped on the new magenta silk robe he'd surprised her with last week. It was unusual for her to beat the alarm clock or to wake up before he did, and she was delighted to be able to sneak down and have his coffee ready for a change.

Over the two months since he'd moved in, he'd consistently had coffee ready by the time she dragged her weary behind downstairs. Sometimes he even brought it up to her while she was still soaking in the bathtub.

This morning she was particularly happy to beat him to it. He hadn't slept most of the night, and she knew better than to think he would sleep late. She hadn't slept much better herself. But she had at least dozed off from time to time, and whenever she'd awakened, he was lying there staring at the ceiling. When he'd see that her eyes were open, he'd pull her close and tell her to go back to sleep.

Something was bothering him. She only hoped it had nothing to do with her big mouth last night.

She brewed a strong pot of his favorite colombian

blend and carried a mug of it upstairs. She found him starting to sit up in bed. The sheets fell to his waist, exposing his bare chest, and her breath caught in her throat, just like it always did when she was struck with the sheer beauty of him.

"Mornin'," he said, trying to stifle a yawn. Smiling, he took the mug she offered, but instead of taking a sip, he put it on the nightstand, grabbed her wrist and pulled her toward him.

"Good morning to you, too." She sank into the sheets, and he rolled her over until he was on top of her. She laughed, dodging the tickling kisses he showered down her neck.

"Trying to get away from me?" he asked between nibbles.

"Your beard—" giggling, she threw her head to one side "—tickles." He was careful not to give her any burns, making sure his kisses were light, which made the sensation all the more ticklish. "Besides, you're going to be late for work."

Sighing heavily, he flopped onto his back, bringing her with him to lay on his chest. "Yeah, work." He scrubbed at his face, keeping one arm around her. "Can you believe there was a time I lived for work? I couldn't wait to get out of bed in the morning. Hell, I must be getting old."

Smiling, Gracie circled a fingertip around his nipple. "Maybe you just have better things to do in bed these days."

"Like what?"

She squinted at the feigned innocence on his face and swatted him.

He laughed, pulling her to his chest, then kissed

her until she couldn't breathe. Within seconds, the silk robe slid to the floor and they lay naked, hugging, kissing, laughing. And then suddenly, without warning, Gracie felt tears well up behind her eyes. Because she knew this was all going to end in a few weeks. And there wasn't a thing she could do about it.

GRACIE STARED at Zoey, feeling a twinge of guilt for not having heard a word her friend had said for the past five minutes. She slowly sipped her cappuccino, her brain scrambling to make sense of why Mrs. Green's hair had not taken the color Zoey had applied. But once again, her thoughts slid to Adam.

She'd been wrong this morning. There sure as heck was something she could do about the end to their story. She had to tell him she loved him, that she didn't want him to leave.

Gracie was certain he felt the same way. Well, fairly certain. Even though he'd never actually said the words, he'd shown how he felt in so many ways, like making sure she always had gas in her car, that it was washed on a regular basis. She'd seen the list of household repairs he intended to make, and each week it had grown longer. He also kept her well-supplied with ice cream, even though she'd complained of gaining three pounds.

She smiled thinking about the night his lips teasingly spent searching for those extra pounds.

"Are you listening?" Zoey asked, frowning, and Gracie's attention snapped to the present.

"Of course. Mrs. Green's hair now matches her name, thanks to you."

"I'm trying to tell you it wasn't my fault." Zoey

glared at Gracie. But after a moment, her expression softened, and she said, "He's the one, isn't he?"

Gracie couldn't help the smile that curved her lips. She wasn't going to deny anything, even if Zoey jumped down her throat. She shrugged. "I'm crazy about him, Zoey. I don't know when it happened, or even how it happened." She shook her head. "I never thought I could feel this way about anyone, much less so soon after Dwight, but it's so…different, it's…it's—"

"Love?" Zoey grinned, looking like a pleased parent while Gracie gaped in shock. "Don't look at me like that. Sure, I was bitchy in the beginning, but I like Adam now. And it's obvious that he adores you."

"You think so?" Gracie's lips stretched so wide she wasn't sure they could ever return to normal.

Zoey rolled her eyes. "Oh, please. The man's got tunnel vision whenever you're in the room. He thinks the sun rises and sets on your butt, and you know it."

Gracie raised furrowed brows. "But he hasn't actually *told* me anything yet."

"Believe me, honey, showing is a hell of a lot better than cheap talk." Zoey signaled for their waitress to refill her cup. She turned to Gracie. "And he shows you, doesn't he?"

"He *seems* to care for me."

Zoey chuckled. "The guy is working long hours, busting his butt to make enough money to last him through winter, and he still finds time to keep your car filled with gas. And I noticed he replaced one of your front steps."

"Yes," Gracie drawled.

Her friend made a face. "I can't believe you can sound even remotely unconvinced. Hell, he wouldn't even take my money."

The last word was barely out of Zoey's mouth when she gasped, her eyes widening. She blinked several times in rapid succession before she dove for her Flintstones lunch pail.

An eerie chill swept Gracie. If not for Zoey's stricken face and the way she was trying desperately to avoid eye contact, she might have ignored the odd comment. But something was wrong. Very wrong. "What money?" Gracie asked slowly.

"I've got to get to the shop," Zoey said, nearly dropping the contents of her wallet as she rushed to leave money for the check. "Millie Snodgrass is my first appointment. She's getting a perm and she can be a real bitch if I make her wait for even a minute."

"What money?" Gracie repeated calmly, her tone firm.

"Nothing, Gracie. Really. You know me, always shooting my mouth off before I think." Zoey yanked out a packet of gum as she stood, her hand shaking as she unwrapped three pieces and started stuffing one after another into her mouth.

"I'd hold off on that," Gracie said, her solemn gaze pinned purposefully on her friend. "It'll be hard to explain with your mouth full."

"I really have to go—"

"Zoey."

"Look, I offered him a loan. He wouldn't take it."

Gracie shook her head, a sudden sadness slowing her movement. "I've seen you lie to other people. I never thought you'd lie to me."

Zoey's shoulders sagged as she sank into her seat. "Oh, Gracie, promise you won't get mad."

"Tell me what happened."

"Will you promise—" Zoey broke off and looked away when she saw the tension building in Gracie's eyes. "I hired him to pay attention to you and make Dwight jealous."

Gracie blinked. Sitting up a little straighter, she took a deep, painful breath. But her lungs couldn't seem to capture enough air. Panicking, she tried to swallow, but her mouth wasn't working, either.

Zoey's anxious gaze flew to her. "Gracie? Are you okay?"

"When?" Odd, her voice sounded normal.

"That morning you told me about Dwight. Gracie? You don't look so hot."

Her hands grew clammy, and they started to tremble, so she folded them in her lap. "The day before I met him?"

"Yeah, but he didn't take the money." Zoey paused, looking uncomfortable. "Well, he did, sort of. But he gave it back."

Gracie glanced at the wall clock. "Millie's waiting."

"Tough." Concern darkened Zoey's eyes. Propping her elbows on the table, she leaned toward Gracie. "Listen, kiddo, it sounds worse than it is. Don't make too much of this. It really never went any further than that morning."

"If you don't get started on Millie's perm, then I'll really be mad because you'll run late all day and we'll miss lunch."

Zoey laughed. "Oh, yeah. Today's ice cream day."

Her gaze briefly searched Gracie's face as she stood. "I'm glad you're handling this okay. Because it really isn't a big deal."

Gracie forced a smile, grateful her friend didn't know that her heart had just shattered into a million pieces.

ADAM AMAZED his entire crew by knocking off work early. That was right after he told them about the new deadline and that he was upping their bonuses to get the job done on time. He'd been generous in his new offer, and he figured it would take the men a while to come down to earth. Tomorrow they'd go back to their breakneck schedule, working double overtime. By the time this job was over, he'd be lucky if he broke even.

He didn't give a rip. He had something more important on his mind.

On the way home he stopped at a florist, then swung by Eduardo's to slip the maître d' fifty bucks for dinner reservations for later. The popular restaurant generally adhered to a waiting list, but Adam didn't want to wait. After a restless night and only a couple hours of sleep, he'd come to the conclusion that he'd done enough waiting.

He wanted to marry Gracie.

When he pulled into the drive, he was relieved to see her car in the garage. As he started to get out of his truck and reach for the roses he'd bought, to his amazement, he noticed that his palms had grown damp.

He took several deep breaths. What if she turned him down? She'd never uttered a word about love, but then neither had he. Although he'd had strong feelings for her for some time, he hadn't been entirely sure until last night. Then the feeling had hit him with all the impact of a wrecking ball.

Discussing his mother with Gracie turned out to be an eye-opener for him. Even though she had backed off, Gracie had known she was right. He'd been an immature, first-class jerk for years. He had been taunting his mother, rubbing her nose in his success. Yet even after seeing that ugly part of him, Gracie had still been on his side. She's said her piece and then she accepted him, faults and all, just like she had accepted the mistaken notion that he was some hand-to-mouth, itinerant handyman. She hadn't criticized. She hadn't judged. Because that wasn't Gracie's way.

His only flimsy excuse for being such a blind ass until now was that he'd never received such unconditional acceptance before. Not from his family, not from anyone. And he wasn't about to throw it all away and become another Dwight by letting the best person who'd ever entered his life slip away.

He didn't want to be another Thomas Carpenter, either, in his seventies and too driven by greed, power and screwed-up priorities to appreciate life. And most of all, he didn't want to be an older version of himself, alone with his petty grudges and missing Gracie.

He wiped one palm down the front of his jeans, transferred the long-stemmed roses to his dry hand, then repeated the process with his other palm. It took him only two tries to get the key in the lock, and as soon as he opened the door, he saw her standing in the kitchen near the window.

Quickly he hid the flowers behind his back and

tried to look casual as he stepped over the threshold into the semidarkness. The only light in the room came from the salmon-tinted twilight streaming in through the window.

"Hi," he said, wondering where his usual welcoming smile was. "I'm glad you're home early."

She didn't say anything, and a creepy feeling slithered across his nerve endings. He stopped halfway, uneasy with her stony silence in the dusky light, and although this wasn't what he had planned, he awkwardly produced the roses from behind his back and held them out to her.

When she didn't make a move to take them, he stepped forward and saw her face clearly for the first time. Even with the gray shadows coloring her expression, he could tell that her eyes were dull, her complexion wan. She looked...devastated.

He threw the roses onto the counter and moved to take her in his arms. "Gracie, is something wrong?"

"Careful," she said, her body so rigid that he dropped his arms, afraid he'd physically hurt her. She glanced at the discarded flowers. "I'd hate to see you damage Zoey's investment."

"Gracie? I don't understand—" His gaze anxiously inspected her body. "Are you hurt?"

She laughed, the sound so brittle, so un-Gracie it unnerved him. "Maybe you should put them in water," she said.

"I don't give a damn about the roses—"

"Right. We don't have an audience." She hugged her ribs tightly as if to ward off a chill. "I think I'll turn up the heat."

When she started to walk past him, he cupped her

elbow in a firm grip and forced her to stop. "Tell me what's wrong. We've always been able to talk about everything. What does this have to do with Zoey?"

Her laugh was strangled, injected with anguish. "I should be asking you that. What was the deal, Adam? How much was my dignity worth to you?"

Closing his eyes, he bowed his head in comprehension. "Zoey told you." When he raised his gaze, raw pain sliced through his heart at the bleakness he saw in Gracie's face. "I would have told you myself, but I didn't think it made a difference anymore."

"Why? Because you'd already slept with me?"

He muttered a vicious curse. "Don't, Gracie. I don't know what Zoey told you, but I guarantee you it's not what you apparently think.

"Honestly, Adam, I don't think anything. I'm too numb to think." She shrugged away from him and headed out of the kitchen. "No, that's not true," she said, slowing without turning. "I think you should leave. Tonight. After you pack your things."

"Gracie, please listen. This wasn't about money. I don't need Zoey's or anyone else's money. I have more money than I can ever spend. I only did it because—"

She glanced briefly at him, holding up a hand, pleading for silence. A shadow veiled her face. "I wish it didn't hurt so much. But it does." She paused, her voice thick. "It hurts a lot, and if you ever cared for me at all, even the tiniest bit, you'll leave right now."

Adam stared helplessly as she slowly lifted her chin and squared her shoulders. He didn't know what to say, what he could do to soothe her wounded pride.

"I'd appreciate it if you left your key on the counter," she said quietly, and moved toward the dining room...away from him...out of his life.

And for the first time he could remember, Adam knew what it was like to feel so incredibly alone.

GRACIE DIDN'T KNOW how she made it up the stairs without stumbling. As soon as she got to her room, she closed the door, and before her knees gave out, she slid to the carpet. Hugging her bent legs, she rocked herself until the motion induced an odd calming effect and she could breathe evenly again. She slowed the action, rested her forehead on her knees and pressed her ear to the door.

She couldn't hear Adam. She couldn't hear anything but a faint buzzing in her head, like an electric circuit on the verge of shorting out. Her entire body was humming, as though it were about to ignite, and she closed her eyes and ordered herself to think about something pleasant and comforting, but an image of Adam popped into her head, and before she could stop herself, she imagined she could feel his strong, callused hands on her body.

She cursed under her breath, expelling a word she'd never used before. She'd only known him for a couple of months. How could it hurt this bad? How could she feel so damn rotten?

Because he'd lied. He'd made her feel attractive and important and cared for. And when she'd finally started to believe, he'd yanked her confidence out from under her. How could she have been so gullible? Hadn't she learned anything from her experience with Dwight?

She staggered to her feet and caught a glimpse of herself in the mirror. To her horror, the old Gracie stared back. The image was enough to shake her, and with sudden clarity, she knew she couldn't go back to being the person she was.

She was no longer the timid person who'd split up with Dwight, the one all too ready to accept more than her share of the blame if it kept the peace. Nor was she the person who'd met Adam, needy, so willing to accept that she wasn't good enough. The truth was, she didn't deserve the lies he'd dished out.

And he didn't deserve her.

She was stronger now. She wasn't going to crumple. She just wished it didn't have to hurt so damn bad.

IT HAD TAKEN Gracie all week to drag the boutique's Christmas decorations out of storage. Although she wouldn't start putting them up until tomorrow, the day before Thanksgiving, she'd started organizing things early because it seemed to take her twice as long to do anything these days.

She hadn't heard from Adam. Not that she had expected or wanted to hear from him. But hurt and confusion were still there and weighed her every moment like two-ton bricks.

Sighing, she glanced wistfully around the store. After ten years, this could very well be her last Christmas here. She'd decided to call Martha's granddaughter's bluff, after all. If she wouldn't at least make Gracie an equal partner, Gracie was tendering her resignation as of the first of the year.

She supposed she had Dwight and Adam to thank

for finally having some confidence and backbone. Because Gracie decided she wasn't going to be pushed around any more. She was smart, capable, resourceful. And one way or another, she would have her own store.

"Christmas. Bah, humbug. The mall closed five minutes ago, and people are still swarming the place like locusts."

Gracie turned when she heard Zoey's voice. "Close the door, would you? I'll get the key."

"Good." Zoey did as she was asked, then pulled on her faux leopard coat as she approached Gracie. "I was hoping we'd get out of here on time. I'm taking you for a drink."

"Not tonight." She reached under the counter for her purse. The cash had already been counted. She was eager to leave, too.

"Come on, Gracie. You said that last night and the night before. You're still mad at me, aren't you?"

She shook her head. "You explained everything. And although I don't agree with what you did, I understand you were just trying to help. But if you do anything like that again, I will definitely tell everyone you're really a blonde."

Wincing, Zoey patted her ebony bob. "If you forgive me, then you forgive Adam, right?"

Gracie didn't answer, partly because she didn't know what to say. Although there was a certain logic to Zoey's conclusion, reality wasn't that simple. Nor was human emotion.

"Look, kiddo, you know me," Zoey continued. "I'd be the last person to defend the guy if I thought for one minute the poor dumb jerk wasn't head over heels in love with you.''

Gracie continued to gather her things without commenting. She'd heard this spiel before. At least five times.

''He's leaving,'' Zoey said, carefully studying Gracie's face. ''The job was completed this morning.''

Gracie stopped what she was doing. ''You talked to him?''

''His men told me.''

''His men?'' Gracie frowned, and forgetting her vow to make not a single inquiry about Adam Knight, she asked, ''What men? What's going on?''

The phone rang, and both women glanced at it. ''Maybe that's him,'' Zoey said.

Gracie moistened her lips. *So what?* She didn't want to talk to him. *Maybe he's calling to say good-bye.* She just wouldn't answer it.

On the fourth ring, she grabbed the receiver, not sure if she wanted it to be him, or not. ''Hello?''

''Ms. Allen, please,'' said a curt male voice on the other end.

After Gracie identified herself, the man said, ''This is Thomas Carpenter. I have your lease papers ready to sign, Ms. Allen. I was supposed to wait until Friday, but I'll be away for the Thanksgiving weekend. Can we meet tomorrow?''

Gracie's gaze flicked to Zoey, and she shrugged at her friend's quizzical expression. ''I think you have the wrong person, Mr. Carpenter. I have no idea what you're talking about.''

There was a moment's hesitation before he said, ''There's no mistake. Mr. Knight's instructions were very emphatic. My secretary will arrange a meeting tomorrow, assuming that's convenient.''

''What does this have to do with Adam?'' She narrowed her irritated gaze at Zoey, who put up both hands in supplication.

Mr. Carpenter's impatient sigh cut through the phone lines. ''Maybe the letter he included will explain. You'll have to take that up with him. But I'll say this. I hope you're a better businessperson than he is, Ms. Allen. The damn fool just gave away the farm.''

GRACIE SAT behind the wheel of her Nissan, not sure she had the energy to get out and climb the two steps to her back door. So much had happened in the past few hours, so much information relayed for her overtaxed brain to absorb, that her head ached. Her wrists crossed on the steering wheel, she dropped her forehead on them for a moment, then slowly turned to stare at the large white envelope sitting on the seat beside her. Her future. All wrapped up in a neat little package.

She should be ecstatic. She was finally getting what she wanted. Not exactly the way she had planned, although she was determined to pay Adam back every cent it had cost him, with interest—inflated interest. She would get an attorney to draw up the documents so the repayment schedule was not only legal but would make their arrangement strictly business.

Her first inclination had been to turn down the store, but the deal between Adam and Mr. Carpenter had already been cut, and if she didn't accept it, according to Adam's terms, the store would sit empty.

Just like she felt right now.

She slammed the heel of her hand against the steering wheel. It wasn't supposed to have turned out this way. Why couldn't she have been big enough to look for Adam sooner, before he'd left town? Why did she have to learn about him from Zoey? And if her friend hadn't felt guilty and hired someone to check him out, Gracie might never have truly known about the man she loved.

Not that it mattered. She didn't care if he was a handyman or some construction magnate. But it did matter that what happened between them had nothing to do with money. And what hurt the most was that her heart had already known that. It was her confidence that had betrayed her, that wouldn't let her believe someone like Adam could truly love her. So she'd blown it.

"Damn. Are you going to sit there all evening? It's cold out here."

She blinked at the sound of his heart-stopping familiar voice. Then she raised her head and stared, wide-eyed, straight ahead, afraid she'd turn to find that it was only her imagination.

"Come on, Gracie, don't leave me standing out here."

Slowly, she swiveled. Adam stood a few feet from her car. His arms were crossed over his chest as he vigorously rubbed the sleeves of his old frayed denim jacket. Swallowing hard, she opened her car door and got out.

She looked past him and saw his truck parked at the curb, the tops of his suitcase and duffel visible through the windshield. "Why did you come back?"

she asked, returning her gaze to him, her voice sounding so calm it amazed her.

His hands slowed until they fell to his sides. "Today is Wednesday." He took a step forward. "I forgot to put out the garbage."

She didn't move. "What about next week?" she asked.

"I'll put it out early."

Hope soared in her chest, and she leaned against the car for support. "You might not be here."

"I will if you let me." He slowly took her hand as if unsure she'd allow him to do so. "I was wrong for not telling you about Zoey and me, but I can't pay for that one mistake for the rest of my life. I swear to God I didn't take a penny from her. Besides, for me it was never about money or making Dwight jealous. I wanted you, Gracie." He shrugged, his eyes staying squarely on her face. "I think from the first moment I saw you smile."

She swallowed. "We haven't known each other that long," she said, wanting to be impulsive but still a little afraid. "What we have is new and exciting. All that newness is going to wear off."

"Only if we let it. I'm not willing to do that. Are you?" he asked, and she shook her head. "Besides, I hate to break it to you, but taking out the garbage is nothing new." He grinned. "I promise to never stop doing that. You can even put it in our marriage vows if you want."

"Marriage?"

"I love you, Gracie," he said, his voice lowering. He kissed her gently, briefly. "I want to marry you, and I want to give you a whole mess of kids to boss around. Will you marry me?''

She laughed. ''Marriage before kids would definitely be a good thing.'' She sobered when he started to smile. ''What about your job?''

He sobered quickly, too. ''That's something else I have to explain. I'm not exactly a handyman. I have—''

''I know.''

His brows shot up.

''Zoey.''

He laughed uneasily. ''Figures.''

''Besides, I met with Mr. Carpenter this afternoon.''

''Damn. He was supposed to call you on Friday.'' Adam's eyes darkened warily. ''Can we consider the store a wedding present, or are you going to chew me out?''

''That depends. We still haven't discussed your job.''

He nodded, looking a little unhappy. ''There are times I'll have to be away until all my contracts are met.''

She nodded. ''I'll have buying trips. We'll make them coincide.''

''Your answer is yes?''

''I want to come home to you, Adam. I'll always want to come home to you.''

He lifted her off the ground and spun her around. ''I love you, Gracie Klutz Allen,'' he shouted.

''I love you, Adam Knight,'' she answered, laughing. ''But you're making me dizzy.''

"Good. You've been making me dizzy for two months. How fast can we get married? Tomorrow?"

"Tomorrow is Thanksgiving," she said breathlessly as he set her down. "Friday, maybe. I'll call Zoey and ask her to be my matron of honor. Then I'll call—"

"Damn. I wanted her to be my best man."

The both laughed. "She and Brian are coming over for dinner tomorrow," Gracie said, hoping there were genuinely no hard feelings between her future husband and her best friend.

"Perfect," Adam said. "I couldn't think of a better way to spend Thanksgiving. That lady's given me a lot to be thankful for," he said, and kissed her like there was no tomorrow, after all.